FORCED MARCH

Also by Leo Kessler

The *SS Assault Regiment Wotan* Series
SS PANZER BATTALION
DEATH'S HEAD
CLAWS OF STEEL
GUNS AT CASSINO
THE DEVIL'S SHIELD
HAMMER OF THE GODS
FORCED MARCH
BLOOD AND ICE
THE SAND PANTHERS
COUNTER-ATTACK
PANZER HUNT
SLAUGHTER GROUND
HELLFIRE
FLASHPOINT
CAULDRON OF BLOOD
SCHIRMER'S HEADHUNTERS
WHORES OF WAR
SCHIRMER'S DEATH LEGION
DEATH RIDE

The *Stormtroop* Series
STORMTROOP
BLOOD MOUNTAIN
VALLEY OF THE ASSASSINS
RED ASSAULT
HIMMLER'S GOLD
FIRE OVER KABUL
WAVE OF TERROR
EAGLES IN THE SNOW
FIRE OVER AFRICA

The *Otto Stahl* Series
OTTO'S PHONEY WAR
OTTO'S BLITZKRIEG!
OTTO AND THE REDS
OTTO AND THE YANKS
OTTO AND THE SS
OTTO AND THE HIMMLER LOVE LETTERS

The *Sea Wolves* Series
SINK THE SCHARNHORST!
DEATH TO THE DEUTSCHLAND

Also:

As Klaus Konrad
The Russian Series
FIRST BLOOD
MARCH ON MOSCOW
FRONT SWINE

LEO KESSLER

FORCED MARCH

Wotan 7

Macdonald

A Macdonald Book

First published in Great Britain in 1976
by Futura Publications, a division of
Macdonald & Co (Publishers) Ltd
London & Sydney

This edition 1984

British Library Cataloguing in Publication Data

Kessler, Leo
    Forced march.—(Wotan; 7)
    Rn: Charles Whiting   I. Title   II. Series
    823'.914 [F]   PR6061.E84/
    ISBN 0–356–10599–7

Printed in Great Britain by
Redwood Burn Limited, Trowbridge, Wiltshire
Bound at The Dorstel Press

Macdonald & Co (Publishers) Ltd
Maxwell House
74 Worship Street
London EC2A 2EN

A BPCC plc Company

'You belong now to SS Assault Battalion Wotan and in the manner of your death you cannot bring dishonour to Wotan. For when you are long forgotten, your idle bones mouldering under some French clod, this Battalion will be remembered. Do you understand that, soldiers?'

The Vulture, CO of SS Battalion Wotan,
Dieppe, France. July 1942.

A SHORT GLOSSARY OF WOTAN TERMS

Full House   Both venereal diseases
Asparagus Tarzan   Weakling
Popov, Ivan   Russian soldier
Dicebeaker   Jackboots
Flatman   Flat bottle of schnapps
Greenbeak, wet-tail   Raw recruit
Ami   American
Base stallion   Rear area soldier, base wallah
Bone-mender   Doctor
Warm brother   Homosexual
Kitchen-bull   Army cook
Dead soldier   Empty bottle
Field Mattress   German Army female auxiliary
Tin   Decorations
Throatache   Knight's Cross of the Iron Cross
Moss   Money
Old Man   Tinned meat
Cancer stick   Cigarette
Giddi-up soup   Horsemeat soup
Stubble-hopper   Infantryman
Reeperbahn equalizer   Brass knuckles
Pavement tail   Street walker
Flipper   Hand
Turnip   Head

BOOK ONE: OPERATION JUBILEE

'Mountbatten, understand this. Failure at Dieppe is what I demand of you!' *Premier Churchill to Lord Louis Mountbatten. July 1942.*

ONE

'Great God and all his triangles!' Sergeant Schulze of SS Battalion Wotan cursed. He raised himself in the field hospital bed and gave one of his well-known farts.

Opposite him in the long ward One-Egg, the young panzer grenadier, who had had his left testicle shot off before Moscow tut-tutted; and next to him the Lung, wounded at the crossing of the River Bug, bubbled a little louder than usual.

'Just letting off a little green smoke, that's all,' Schulze mumbled, and tried to scratch the end of his big nose, but without success. This was not surprising, since both his hands were enclosed in thick plaster up to the wrists: the result of his being rather slow in getting rid of a Soviet stick grenade in the confused hand-to-hand fighting just outside Kiev.

In the next bed Matz's springs squeaked as he turned round painfully. 'What's shitting you now, Schulze?' he demanded.

Schulze looked across at his running mate from Wotan. Matz's blond hair was hopelessly matted; he hadn't shaved since the hospital train had delivered them at Berlin's *Lar Charite* Hospital from the front two weeks ago; and cigar ash lay over the blue and white striped cover like snow. 'Are you addressing me, Corporal?' he asked severely.

'Who do you think, you big soft wet-tail? Winston shitty Spencer shitty Churchill?'

'Put a "sergeant" on that Schulze, Corporal,' barked Schulze. 'And remember to show a bit more respect for a wounded NCO, or I'll take that pegleg of yours' – he indicated Matz's artificial limb hanging over the edge of the white hospital bed – 'and stick it so far up yer ass that yer eyes'll pop out!'

11

'All right, *Sergeant* Schulze. What's up? What yer belly-aching about? We're in a nice safe hospital a thousand kilo-metres behind the front, with no hairy-assed Popovs trying to shoot the eggs off'n us. What more do you want, *Sergeant* Schulze?'

'I want out of here, Matz, that's what I want. I'm brassed off by this place. No fucking sauce — that big bone-mender took my last flatman off me this morning. No fucking tail. And no fucking Wotan!' The big ex-docker sighed sadly. 'We've been abandoned by the Battalion, Matz. At the mercy of these banana-sucking bone-mender's, every one of them a warm brother, if you ask me. Me with two useless flippers and you with one sodding leg already off and the other likely be sabred off any day now the way those asparagus Tarzans of medics are carrying on.' Schulze hawked miserably and directed a gob of phlegm into the brass spitoon in the centre of the long ward.

Sister Klara, the ugly Red Cross nurse in her forties who was now washing the panzer grenadier's lower body, looked angrily up from her task. 'I forbid you to do that in my presence, Sergeant,' she said severely, 'and watch your langu-age, or I'll have to talk to the chief doctor about your be-haviour.' She sniffed self-righteously and turned back to her task. The panzer grenadier closed his eyes again in blissful ecstasy.

'That's what happens to an ugly woman, Matzi,' Schulze said, responding to the challenge. 'I mean an ugly bloke can go out and buy himself a piece of that pavement tail down there on the *Kudamm*.* But yer ugly woman — what can she do? She can't buy it.' He shrugged and winced with the pain. 'All she can do is finger herself crazy.'

Sister Klara, still busy washing the panzer grenadier's lower body, flushed scarlet. An amused Schulze could see the blush creeping down her scraggy neck under the severe bun.

* Famous Berlin thoroughfare. (Transl.)

'Of course in France they have houses for that kind of woman,' Matz volunteered, joining in the game.

'What?'

'Knocking shops for ugly women.'

Schulze's broad face contorted in mock disgust. '*What a piggery!*' he exclaimed. 'Trust those filthy frogs. Think of any dirty perversion and you'll find, Matzi, that the Frogs invented it. No wonder the Führer in his infinite wisdom did them the favour of occupying their shitting country two years ago – learn them a bit of German decency. I mean Matzi, fancy being forced to stick that little bit o' meat of yours into that – even for money!' He shuddered melodramatically.

'To be honest, Schulze,' Matz said, as if he were seriously considering the proposition. 'I wouldn't exactly say no. The old five-fingered widow's getting very slack now.'

'It's all right for you, Matzi,' Schulze grunted mournfully. 'With these flippers of mine tied up like this, I can't even enjoy a bit of the old five-fingered widow. I mean look over there. One-Egg's doing himself a bit of all right,' he indicated the panzer grenadier, his mouth wide open, breathing fast as Sister Klara washed carefully around his genitals. 'Even he's getting a cheap thrill.'

'And I bet she is too,' Matz added maliciously, his little eyes sparkling wickedly. 'Look how she's holding his peterman. Yer'd think she's handling the Prussian crown jewels the way she's got hold of it. Great crap on the Christmas Tree – I bet she's at it tonight like a fiddler's elbow once she gets into her little bed. *Grr!*' The little Corporal growled throatily.

This was too much for Sister Klara. She dropped her washcloth over the panzer grenadier's penis. 'I shall report you to the Chief,' she said thickly through her tears. 'He'll see that you two foul-mouthed beasts land where you belong – in the punishment ward!' And with that she was gone, leaving the panzer grenadier staring disconsolately at the wash cloth.

Schulze looked at Matz mockingly. 'Now what was that in

13

aid of, Matzi?' he asked. 'Did we say something?'

But before Matz could reply, the first thin wail of the air raid sirens outside indicated that the RAF would soon be paying one of its nightly visits to Berlin.

'Red alert,' Matz said. 'The Tommies'll be over soon, dropping their square eggs as usual, the pigs.'

Schulze did not seem to hear. 'We're off, Matzi,' he announced abruptly. 'That ugly cow's not putting me in the punishment ward, drinking cold nigger sweat and eating lousy giddi-up soup. No thank you. We're off!'

'But where?' Matz protested.

Schulze sucked his big yellow teeth thoughtfully. 'First we'll sink a *Korn* – perhaps two. Then a bit of that pavement tail to get rid of the dirty water from our chests. Mine's already up to my throat. If I don't get a bit of the other soon, it'll choke me. Then we're off to find the Wotan.'

Matz looked at the big sergeant incredulously. 'Have you got all yer cups in yer cupboard, Schulze? How we gonna get out of here? You with yer flaming flippers and me with my sodding foot. I can't walk, you know that.'

'Don't wet yer skivvies, Matzi,' Schulze answered easily. 'I'll soon fix that.' He raised his voice. 'Hey, you One-Egg! Get yer paws off'n that disgusting bit of meat of yours and wheel in that hospital panzer from the corridor – at the double!'

'But I'm badly wounded in the groin,' protested One-Egg.

'You'll be *very* badly wounded in the ass if you don't move it, One-Egg.'

The threat worked. Painfully One-Egg heaved himself out of the bed and shuffled to the door, holding his hands protectively to his abdomen.

'If you drop it, I'll yell out!' Matz cried after him.

'Button that lip, Matzi,' Schulze ordered impatiently, 'and pass me that sabre of yours.'

Obediently the one-legged SS man reached across his ceremonial NCO's dagger. Schulze grabbed at it clumsily and holding it between his two white plaster paws, began sawing through the cord holding up Matz's one remaining leg. Finally he managed to cut through it. Matz's wounded foot, swathed in thick bandages crashed to the bed.

'Heaven, arse and twine,' Matz cursed, 'can't you be a bit more careful, you big horned ox! That shitting well hurt!'

'Crap in yer cap, cripple!' Schulze snapped unfeelingly, awkwardly tucking his long hospital nightshirt into the top of his black pants. 'You seem to forget that you're talking to a non-commissioned officer of the Greater German Army. Pass me my dicebeakers, will yer.'

As Matz struggled to reach Schulze's jackboots, One-Egg opened the door to the ward and trundled in the ancient wicker-work bathchair. His young face was an ashen-grey. 'I think it's opened up again – the wound, I mean,' he said sorrowfully.

'Well, don't take long strides then,' Schulze rapped without sympathy, 'or yer other egg might fall out of its little nest. Come on, don't stand there like a fart in a trance! Give me a hand to get this little cripple into his pram.'

'But where in three devils' name are you going?' One-Egg asked, his curiosity overcoming his pain, as he helped Schulze to lower Matz into the bathchair.

'Where are we going?' Schulze echoed. 'We're gonna do a three-F.'

'What?'

'Christ on a crutch, One-Egg, you still got eggshell behind yer spoons or something – find it, feel it and ferk it, man!'

'Oh,' One-Egg answered, 'and then, Schulzi?'

'Then, my little battered balls of a panzer grenadier,' Schulze cried, 'we're off to find the finest battalion in the whole Greater German Army – *SS Battalion Wotan!*' A moment later he was gone through the swinging doors, pushing Matz in front of him like an evil wizened baby.

15

TWO

'May the Almighty have mercy upon us!' Matz breathed as Schulze pushed him through the throng of excited, loud field-greys waiting for their turn to go upstairs. The great 19th-century salon with its red-plush over-stuffed furniture was packed with whores in their multi-coloured crêpe-de-chine underwear. Red-faced sweating maids were running every-where, bearing silver trays of cigarettes and bottles. The place was obviously doing boom business despite the bombs crashing to the ground outside.

'Cast one of your glassy orbs on all that nooky,' Schulze sighed. 'Grr, Matzi, it's so good I could eat it with a knife and fork – and no salt!' And listen to those springs going upstairs. Ain't that beautiful music – better than the *Horst Wessel Lied* and *Deutschland über Alles* both put together!'

'Look at that one,' Matz said, pointing to a huge blonde whore, whose massive breasts were threatening to burst out of her gleaming black slip. 'The wood she's got in front of her door!' Carried away by his enthusiasm, he reached out two greedy hands to seize the blonde.

But a hulking artilleryman with the peaked cap and sun-tanned face of the *Afrika Korps* pushed in front of him. 'Keep yer paws off'n her, you one-legged cripple!' he snarled. 'You wait yer turn like the rest of us. I haven't seen a white woman for a month of Sundays. Hold it in yer shitty hand if yer in a hurry. That puny little thing you've probably got won't be much to these girls anyway.'

There was a flutter of laughter from the waiting soldiers. While Matz stuttered with rage, Schulze looked the big *Afrika Korps* artilleryman up and down coldly. 'Do you know whom

16

you are addressing, you chimney-sweep run wild?' he asked with frosty politeness. 'No, then I shall inform you. You are speaking with a non-commissioned officer of the finest battalion of the finest division in the Armed SS. Namely SS Battalion Wotan of the Adolf Hitler Bodyguard Division.'

The artilleryman was not impressed. 'I'd like to ask you something?'

'Please.'

'I'd like to know, whether your mother was a virgin or not when you were born?' he asked with a sneer. 'Or did they find you under a cabbage leaf?'

His sally earned him another burst of laughter from the impatient soldiery. The blonde giggled so much that her right breast flopped out of its black cage. The soldiers whistled and cheered loudly.

Schulze waited till the whistling had died down, controlling himself with difficulty. 'Pop to!' he barked as if he were back on the Battalion's parade ground. 'Heave up those juiceless ribs! Grind that jaw! Smear that big turnip of yours against the back of your collar! You're talking to an SS non-commissioned officer, man!'

'Sewer Stomach!' grunted the artilleryman.

'I'm going to shear off your ass for those insidious words, soldier,' Schulze threatened, his big face flushing crimson. 'Dirty fart-cannon –'

Before Schulze could hit the grinning artilleryman, Matz brought up his artificial leg. The booted foot caught him between his legs. He screamed and sank to his knees. Calmly Schulze brought his clenched plaster hands down on the back of the artillerymen's bent head. He fell soundlessly, face down on the carpet.

Grinning triumphantly, the big NCO pushed Matz through the sudden corridor which had opened up between the ranks of the field-greys, nodding grandly to each side like the Führer

17

making his annual triumphal entrance at the Nuremberg Party Day.

The Madame barred their way. Her bosom was thrust underneath her double chin as if she were carrying it on a tray.

'Get a load of that,' Matz cracked. 'What a marvel of engineering! It's better than the Cologne bridge across the Rhine.'

Schulze eyed the Madame's massive bust with naked admiration. 'All that meat and no potatoes – *whew*!'

The Madame wasn't impressed. 'What are yer doing with that shitty pram in my establishment?' she demanded. 'That'll cost you more moss – green moss.' She made her meaning quite clear with a quick gesture of her pudgy be-ringed hand. 'Moss, and then you can park it and have a look at the girls.'

'Show her, Matzi,' Schulze commanded.

'We've got something better than moss, Madame,' Matz said eagerly and digging into the compartment beneath the bathchair, started bringing out the things they had looted on their way out of *La Charité*. 'Three tins of Old Man rations, a cartoon of cancer sticks, one kilo of nigger sweat – and this.' He held up the brown bottle. 'Joy juice.'

'Morphine?' she demanded greedily, her eyes flickering. Like everyone else in the third year of war she knew that the drug brought a fortune on the Berlin black market. The capital was full of wrecked men and women, victims of the battlefield and the home front who only survived by virtue of their daily injection.

'Right in one,' Schulze replied. 'That should do the trick, Madame, eh?'

It did. Within minutes the two of them found themselves half carried upstairs by two of Madame's best girls, the Austrian twins Mitzi and Gerdi and ushered into the brothel's most luxurious room. 'Usually we only let officers and gentlemen in here,' Madame explained, clutching the bottle of morphine tightly to her magnificent breast.

'*Grosse Klasse!*' Matz exclaimed in delight, as the two half-naked whores deposited him on the big bed in the corner. 'Just like heaven.'

Schulze was not so easily pleased. 'It's all right for him, Madame,' he declared. 'The little cripple hasn't got very much to put there in the first place, and in the second, he's a straight up-and-down lover.' He thrust a white stiff paw at his own broad chest. 'Now *I* need more room.' He leered lecherously at Mitzi. 'You see, darling, I'm a real mattress matador. From the side. A nice little movement from the back. And when I'm on top of my form and have use of my flippers I can do it very fine from this way.' He winked and made his meaning very clear. The girls giggled and Schulze slapped the Madame on her generous silk-clad rump. 'But for tonight and under these special circumstances I'll let it go for once. I'll accept the bed – and don't worry, little mother, I'm gentle with virgins.'

Five minutes later Mitzi had pulled off Schulze's dice-beakers and black slacks and was running her delightful snub little Viennese nose along the length of his erect penis, as if she were smelling some particularly beautiful flower, when in the other bed Matz moaned suddenly.

'Schulze!'

'What is it, you stupid bastard?' Schulze demanded angrily. 'Can't you see you're putting me off my stroke?'

'But I can't ... can't –'

'Can't what?'

'Can't get on her!' the little one-legged corporal answered tearfully.

With a muttered curse Schulze turned round. In the dim red light, he could make out Matz's girl naked on the bed, her slim brown legs clutched in her hands high above her head expectantly. Matz, however, was still sitting on his chair, naked and obviously very ready for the task ahead, drooling at the sight.

'She's gonna get a very bad cold with her legs open to the draught like that,' Schulze commented.

'Please Schulzi, no jokes!' Matz pleaded, his eyes desperate. 'I've been dreaming of this for months.'

Schulze jumped off the bed. Hastily he padded across the room on his bare feet, his instrument stuck out in front of him like a cop's club. 'Come on, yer lousy perverted little cripple.' With one sweep of his bandaged hands he gathered up the one-legged corporal and deposited him in the cradle of the girl's legs. 'Now try that one for size,' he growled.

The whore grunted with pleasure and Matz went into action at once, the bedsprings squeaking like red-hot engine pistons.

Schulze wasted no further time either. Outside the bombs were beginning to fall thick and fast. With every fresh explosion, Mitzi gave a delightful little start that added to his pleasure immensely. He took advantage of it, the sweat flooding from his big muscular back.

From the other bed, Matz cried in wild exuberance, 'Race yer Schulzi – race yer, yer old bastard.'

*   *   *

'Stehenbleiben!'

The elegant, monocled staff officer reined back his black mount in alarm. 'In three devils' name, what are you men up to?' he stuttered, his left eye bulging behind the monocle at the sight of a one-legged drunken soldier sprawled in a nightshirt in his bathchair, clutching a chamber-pot full of brown liquid, with a pair of red lace pants on his shaven head, being pushed by an equally drunken brute of a fellow, his flies unbuttoned, his hands encased in plaster and a wooden leg stuck over his shoulder.

'Taking the morning air,' Schulze said helpfully. 'It's very nice now the Tommies have unloaded their square eggs and gone.'

'Fine morning!' the elegant staff officer exploded. 'Man, it's drizzling!'

Schulze looked up and vaguely felt the raindrops on his broad tough face. 'So it is, sir. Didn't notice. Hey, Matzi, put yer hand over me beer. God's pissing in it!'

'Blasphemy, too!' the officer bellowed and reined in his mount. 'What in the name of God is the Armed SS coming to?'

'Shit in the wind!' Matz said drunkenly and took another drink of the stale beer that they had brought with them from the brothel an hour before – 'to keep us fit while we're looking for the Wotan. Shitty warm brother on a shitty old nag!'

'What did you say?'

'Don't take him serious, sir,' Schulze tried to placate the red-faced officer. 'They've got to pump the urine out of him every two hours – that's why he's carrying the piss – er chamberpot. It makes him light-headed. The weight being lifted, you see.'

The officer choked. Stretching his neck out of his tight collar like a strangulated ostrich, he gasped: 'Will you shut up! That man, he ... he insulted me!'

'Insulted you,' Matz inquired with drunken innocence. 'All I said was shit in the wind. Now I don't call that insulting anybody. If I really wanted –'

The rest of his words were drowned by the officer's shrill whistle as he blew the silver alarm pipe hanging from his tunic, his face crimson with rage.

The chain dogs appeared as if from nowhere, four of them led by a sergeant, and all of them armed with carbines. The NCO snapped to attention in front of the officer, the silver crescent plate of his office gleaming in the red ball of the sun which was now beginning to shine through the smoke of the raid. 'Sir?' he rapped.

'Arrest those two disgusting animals,' the officer spluttered. 'Arrest them at once. They have just insulted me – an officer of the Greater General Staff.'

The burly chain dog eyed Schulze warily out of the corner

of his cold eyes, taking in the chestful of decorations and the Knight's Cross of the Iron Cross hanging askew from around his open neck. 'What exactly did they say, sir?' he asked.

The staff officer began to explain while Matz laughed uproariously, threatening to fall out of the ancient bathchair more than once.

'Shit in the wind, the little one said, Sergeant,' the officer concluded, trembling with rage now, 'shit in the wind to an officer of the Greater General St –'

It was then that Matz threw the chamberpot full of stale beer at the officer, soaking the front of his elegant tunic.

'Now look what he's done!' the officer screamed, beating off the liquid with his grey leather glove, as if it were concentrated sulphuric acid, 'he's thrown a pot full of piss at me!'

The chain dogs crowded in on the two SS men. Schulze raised the wooden leg protectively. The big sergeant unslung his carbine. Another chain dog clicked off his safety threateningly. 'You'd better come quietly,' the sergeant commanded. He took a step forward, big hand outstretched to grab Schulze.

But that wasn't to be. With a sudden squeal of brakes a big black Horch came skidding to a halt on the wet cobbles. Huge black-uniformed SS adjutants, every man of them a head taller than Schulze, sprang from the running boards and faced outwards grease-guns at the ready. The sergeant dropped his hand. All around him his men stiffened to attention as they recognised the stiff metal standard flying from the Horch's bonnet.

'Christ on a crutch,' Schulze breathed, as the back door of the big car opened for a portly man with a sallow face and a pair of schoolmaster's pince-nez, his black general's tunic devoid of any decoration save the bronze Sport Medal, third class, 'It's the *Reichsheini* himsen!'

'What is the matter here?' inquired the most feared man in Europe. 'Why are you brawling with my SS men in the middle of Berlin?' Reichsführer SS Heinrich Himmler's dark eyes filled with a genuine look of concern. 'And both of them wounded too!'

'GVHs,'* Schulze snapped. 'But they can't make us KVs† a moment too soon, Reichsführer. We're ready to go back to the front as soon as possible.' He attempted to click to attention, but drunk as he was, he nearly fell over.

Himmler's eyes sparkled warmly. 'That's what I like to hear from my loyal SS men.'

'But Reichsführer,' the staff officer tried to protest.

Himmler withered him with an icy glance. The staff officer's horse seemed to be as frightened by the look as his master and fidgeted restlessly. Reichsführer SS Himmler tut-tutted impatiently. Then his eyes fell on Gerdi's red panties which adorned Matz's shaven skull. 'But why are you wearing what appears to be a – er – female undergarment on your head?' he asked.

Matz, suddenly aware of the fix they were in and not wishing to be sent to the feared Torgau Military Prison from which he had volunteered for the SS, lied glibly. 'It's because of the blood, Reichsführer.'

'Blood?'

'Yes sir. You see it's nearly a month ago since I was wounded, but it still keeps bleeding. The bone-mend – er – doctors can't seem to stop it. So when my comrade here pushes me out for my morning walk in the fresh air, I wear the garment so that the civvies don't see the blood. I feel, Reichsführer, that it would be bad for morale to see a bleeding soldier in the middle of the Reich's capital.

'Laudable, highly laudable,' Himmler said thickly and dabbed his suddenly moist eyes – he was a very emotional man in matters which concerned his elite formation. 'You base stallions who have all the time in the world to go riding when the Reich is in danger from all sides should take an example from

* GVH: *Garnisonverwendungsfahigheimat*, ie fit for home duties.
† KV: *Kriegsverwendungsfahig*, ie fit for frontline duty.

my brave, suffering SS men.'

'Yessir,' gulped the staff officer.

Himmler dismissed him with a wave of his hand then turned to the two SS men again, his sallow face set in a soft smile. 'And now, what can I do for you two heroes?'

Schulze jumped at the opportunity. Even in his drunken stupor, he knew it was the chance he had been looking for these last few days: a means of escaping the white clinical boredom of *La Charité*. 'Reichsführer, we would like to return to our battalion at once.'

'Name?'

'SS Battalion Wotan,' Schulze bellowed, as if he were back on the parade ground at Sennestadt.

Himmler smiled fondly. 'Ah, Wotan,' he exclaimed, 'I have heard very good things about your battalion.'

Nevertheless Schulze thought he noticed a furtive look of hesitation in the Reichsführer's eyes, as he beckoned Schulze to come a little closer. 'Your unit is at Dieppe, Sergeant,' he said softly.

'Dieppe, Reichsführer?'

'On the French coast,' Himmler explained.

'But there's no front there, Reichsführer,' Schulze said, puzzled. 'And there hasn't been ever since the Frogs surrendered two years ago. Wotan is the Führer's Fire Brigade, we're always where the action is.'

Heinrich Himmler winked, an unusual gesture in such a humourless man. 'Don't worry, my brave Sergeant,' he murmured confidentially, 'the Tommies will be taking care of that problem soon.'

THREE

The British Prime Minister wallowed in the bubble bath. 'Well Mountbatten,' he demanded, 'what news of the operation?'

The handsome young aristocratic head of Combined Operations seized his opportunity. New to his important job since the sinking of HMS *Kelly** had left him without a command, he wanted to make instant success of it, as he had done with everything else in his meteoric wartime career. 'I'm afraid, Prime Minister, that the Boche seem to be on to something. Our friends of the Resistance inform us that the Boche are moving in elements of a new panzer division into the area and two units of the Adolf Hitler Bodyguard have been spotted in the Rouen area. They were badly hit in Russia according to our Intelligence and are reforming at the moment. Then yesterday evening we picked this up from Radio Paris: Roosevelt has given Hopkins and Marshall† full power to provide Great Britain with all the help she might need to try a second Narvik, short of sending American troops of course. Churchill should be warned that in attempting a second Narvik, he risks a second Dunkirk.' Mountbatten looked up. 'It might mean they're guessing we're going to have another crack at Norway.' He shrugged slightly. 'Or it could mean, Prime Minister, that they *knew* we're really heading for France.'

Churchill did not speak. His face remained expressionless, almost as if he had been expecting the news. Mountbatten licked his lips and waited for the Prime Minister to speak. But Churchill remained obstinately silent.

* The destroyer he commanded which was sunk off Crete.
* Roosevelt's special advisor, and the Chief of the US Army.

25

In the end, Mountbatten spoke himself. 'Of course, the Boche might simply be doing a little bit of inspired guesswork, Prime Minister. Though we must take into account the fact the op has been on since April, and Field Security has clear proof that the Canadians have been talking about it openly in their pubs on the South-East coast.' He smiled thinly, showing his excellent teeth. 'Our Colonials are a somewhat loud-mouthed bunch, I'm afraid.'

Churchill sat up suddenly. He dipped the end of his cigar into the big jigger of brandy conveniently located at the edge of the bath and stared belligerently at the youthful Head of Combined Operations. Mountbatten told himself that the PM looked like the Chinese God of Plenty with a severe case of bellyache.

'You know why we are putting this op of yours in, don't you, Mountbatten?' he demanded suddenly.

'Well, sir, we haven't done anything since the big Nazaire raid in March, and to use your own words, "the hand of steel, which comes from the sea, and plucks the German sentries from their posts" has been rather idle of late.' He grinned disarmingly.

Churchill glared back. 'It's more than a raid, Mountbatten, *much more*!' he growled, pointing his big cigar at the sailor. 'The Reds are kicking up a devil of a fuss about their losses and how they are bearing the brunt of the fighting. Only last week Uncle Joe* stated publicly that the Red Army has no desire to exterminate the German nation, nor destroy the German state. A perfectly clear indication that the Red bugger is prepared to make a separate peace with Hitler if the situation in Russia gets any worse. Naturally President Roosevelt is worried, that's why he is forcing that new chap of his in Grosvenor Square, General Eisenstein –'

'Eisen*hower*, *General Eisenhower*!'

'Yes, some sort of un-English name like that. Well, he's now

* Nickname for the Soviet dictator Stalin.

busy, at Roosevelt's request, drawing up plans for an invasion this year. *Second Front Now*, you've seen the Communist signs painted everywhere on the walls between here at Chequers and London?'

Mountbatten nodded. Overnight there had been a sudden rash of the signs sprawled in glaring white paint on every available wall. They were obviously the work of the British CP.

'But who will bear the brunt of that invasion, Mountbatten?' Churchill thrust out his pugnacious chin and stared accusingly at the naval officer. 'The British Army. Mountbatten, I would not be doing my duty to my Monarch if I let a new British Army be slaughtered in France. It has taken us two years since Dunkirk to train those ten new divisions and I'm not going to have them thrown into a great battle for which they are not properly prepared, and faced by a German superiority of two and a half divisions to one in France. The British Army will not suffer another defeat on the beaches of France in 1942.

'But my ally demands a landing in Europe this year. There is no way round it, Mountbatten. I have given my word to Roosevelt that they – he and that monster Stalin – will have it. Oh, yes they will get their landing in France in 1942!' He blew a smoke ring slowly into the air above the big bath and said softly. 'Mountbatten, I want a sacrifice from your commandos and the Canadians who will go in with them.'

'A sacrifice?'

Churchill looked at him carefully through half closed eyes. 'Mountbatten, I knew your father. He was able and ambitious like you. But he lacked one thing – political savoir faire. And it was that which ruined him. He was unable to see the way things were going in time and ally himself to a powerful political figure. It ruined his career.'

Mountbatten remained silent, knowing that Churchill was right. His father's German name of Battenberg, which had

27

roused the ire of the hysterical anti-German mob at the start of World War One, had been only part of the reason why he had been forced to resign from the Royal Navy. Papa had also found himself completely isolated politically when the mob had demanded he should go. His father's ruin had been an object lesson for him throughout his naval career and now that war seemed to be opening up hitherto undreamed-of possibilities for him, he was beginning to realise that he would also need powerful friends at court when the time came for him to make the next jump upwards.

'I know you will not make the same mistake as your father.'

'I hope not, sir,' Mountbatten replied, vaguely uneasy at the direction the conversation was taking.

'Good, then we understand each other. As I say then, my American ally must have his landing so that he is prepared to take over the task of placating the Russian bear. But Mountbatten, that landing must show our American ally just how bloody and wasteful of human life an undertaking of that kind is. Roosevelt must be convinced that a second front this summer is absolutely out of the question. My boy, the future of the British Empire might well depend upon the outcome of this operation. If the British Army were to be destroyed this summer, we would never be capable of producing another one – the barrel is about scraped clean and you can imagine what our fate would be in the years to come? For remember, God is always on the side of the big battalions.'

'But, sir, you can't expect me to send in –'

Churchill cut him short with an imperious wave of his hand. 'Mountbatten, understand this. Failure at Dieppe is what I demand of you!'

FOUR

'*Morning, soldiers!*' yelled Colonel Geier above the roar of the waves hitting the base of the French cliffs upon which SS Battalion Wotan now stood rigidly to attention.

'*Morning, Colonel!*' eight hundred hoarse young throats roared back, sending the seagulls sailing away in alarm into the hard blue summer sky above the sea.

'Stand the men at ease please, Sergeant-Major.'

Sergeant-Major Metzger wheeled on his heel. He took up his position in the centre of the hollow square, boots wide apart, chest and jaw thrust out, beefy butcher's hands on his hips. It was a pose he had once seen in an old film about the Kaiser's Army and he had practised it secretly in front of the full-length mirror in his married quarter until he had it perfect. He savoured the moment, running his eyes along the Battalion's rigid ranks. But not one of the men, new recruits as well as the old hands who had survived the Russian carnage, gave him cause for complaint. Every single man was standing woodenly to attention in the prescribed position, eyes fixed hypnotically on the distant horizon. 'Shitehawks,' he told himself, 'yer'd think the dummies were trying to see to England.'

'Stand at ease – *stand easy*,' he bellowed and set the gulls sailing off into the sky again.

Eight hundred right feet shot out at the regulation angle. Eight hundred sets of eyes came back to life and eight hundred men breathed normally once more. In the rear rank someone farted. Metzger flushed. He took the fart as a deliberate insult to himself, as he did everything that went wrong on parade.

The Vulture stared at the Battalion with his ice-blue eyes and slapped his riding cane against the side of his gleaming

29

boots, which, with his grey breeches and their cowhide inlet, clearly marked him as the Regular Cavalry officer that he had been before he had transferred to the newly established Armed SS in order to obtain more rapid promotion. 'Soldiers,' he said impatiently in his thin rasping Prussian voice, 'Wotan is now back up to full combat strength, thanks to our young comrades of the Hitler Youth.' He indicated the 200-strong company of blonde giants temporarily commanded by his second-in-command Major Kuno von Dodenburg. 'Every one a former youth leader, a volunteer and under the legal age for conscription. Seventeen every one of them – a sweet age, in my opinion.' The Vulture smiled thinly and stroked the monstrous abomination of a nose which with his surname* had given him his nickname of Vulture.

Metzger, who knew his CO's little aberration, sniffed and muttered, 'I bet it is for him, the lousy warm brother.' But the big Sergeant-Major was very careful to keep his opinion low.

'We are now in France,' the Vulture said unnecessarily, 'and perhaps some of you older soldiers think that this will be an opportunity for you to laze, amuse yourself with the ladies of easy virtue in Rouen, fill your skins with beer every night. In general, live like gods in France, as the saying goes.' The Vulture's thin mouth snapped open, as if it were worked by steel springs. 'If some of you think like that, then you will be sadly wrong.' He pointed his riding whip challengingly at them. 'Oh yes you will. All of you, old soldiers and new recruits, are here to train and train again for the task that will soon face you. And do you know why I shall train you so hard for an early death, for die you certainly will,' he paused a moment and searched their faces for any sign of weakness or fear. But there was none, for the eight hundred men facing him were the elite of the elite.

The Vulture answered his own question. 'Because you belong to SS Assault Battalion Wotan and in the manner of your

* *Geier* in German means vulture. (Transl.)

30

death you cannot bring dishonour to Wotan. For when you are long forgotten, your idle bones mouldering under some French clod, this Battalion will be remembered. Do you understand that, soldiers?'

'*We understand, Colonel,*' the great cry from eight hundred fervent throats came back in a tremendous roar, as if the elite of National Socialist Germany were impatient to die.

'Good, very good,' said the Vulture and then without warning cried. '*Down!*'

The Battalion dropped on to the still wet grass as one and lay there rigid.

For a moment the Vulture was silent. There was no sound save the crash of the waves, as he let the chill wetness penetrate their thin summer uniforms and soak into their young hard bodies. 'Do you feel it, soldiers – the icy cold of death creeping into your brittle bones. *Do you?*'

'We do, Colonel!' they yelled in unison, not raising their helmeted heads from the wet turf.

'Then savour it, soldiers. For that final, eternal rest will be the only one you will ever enjoy while you are with Wotan ... *Now on your feet!*'

Like the automatons they were, the young SS sprang to their feet, automatically assuming the wooden position of attention, their eyes fixed hypnotically again on the far horizon.

The Vulture swung round. 'Sarnt-Major!'

'Sir!'

'Take them away! Training must commence at once. Do you hear,' the Vulture's voice rose hysterically, 'at once!'

'Sir!'

*   *   *

Major Kuno von Dodenburg, the tall blond aristocratic second-in-command of Wotan, sighed with relief as the Vulture disappeared at his usual rapid pace, then turned to face his new command. For a moment he stared at their innocent yet hard faces and felt a warm surge of pride that National Socialist Germany could still produce such men in the third year of the war. Since 1939 he had seen three drafts pass through Wotan's ranks to disappear for ever into the bloody maws of the terrible war machine. But in all that time he had never seen a group of young men like these. Everyone a Nordic giant, a Hitler Youth leader, who had served the Führer unquestioningly since he was ten years old. Truly an elite of the elite.

Now Reichsführer Himmler was going to realise a long-time dream with these seventeen-year-old volunteers. In due course he would form a whole division of such men, dedicated totally to the Führer, with not a soldier in it, save the senior commanders,* over the age of 21. These men now facing him would one day form the cadre of the First SS Battalion of the new Hitler Youth Division; and Kuno von Dodenburg knew he could not completely consign such highly valuable human material to Metzger's unthinking brutality or the Vulture's cold-blooded cynicism. That was why he had asked the CO to let him take over the company temporarily while they were in training.

'Soldiers, *comrades*,' he began a little awkwardly. 'I welcome you to the First Company of SS Assault Battalion Wotan.'

'Thank you, Major!' they chanted in throaty appreciation.

'You have just heard the Colonel's words. He is a remarkable soldier: the victor of Fort Eben Emael and the crossing of the River Bug.* But you should not always take him so seriously. He is given to – er – an extravagant turn of phrase.' He smiled gently at the young men.

* In fact, the second commander of the Division, 'Panzermeyer' was aged exactly 33, the youngest general in the German Army at that time. (Transl.)

* See SS Panzer Battalion and Death's Head.

They smiled back, relieved to know that the Vulture's promise that they would all die was not to be taken so seriously after all, immediately liking the handsome young officer with the quiet face, clad in a black leather jacket decorated only at the throat by the gleaming Knight's Cross of the Iron Cross.

'Your purpose here,' von Dodenburg said, raising his voice, 'is to be trained *not* how to die, but how to live! And that is why I am going to take a special interest in this company over the next few weeks. Every man of you is a future officer or NCO. As leaders you will have to be ten times tougher than the men under your command. That is why Number One Company is going to perform ten times better than the other three companies. Do you understand, comrades?'

'We understand Major!'

'Good. One last thing. Your training will be hard, very hard, but fair. If any one of you thinks otherwise, he can talk to me at any time – day or night.' He swung round to a waiting Sergeant Metzger. 'All right, Metzger, take them over the Battalion Assault Course – *twice*!'

It was the moment that Metzger, or the Butcher, as the volunteers of the First Company would soon be calling him, had been waiting for. His little piglike eyes gleamed evilly. Ever since the volunteers had arrived at the camp on the cliffs, he had hated them – 'a lot of shitty soft boy scouts in short pants,' he had called them privately to his drinking cronies of the Sergeants' Mess. Now he would make them sweat blood.

'*At your command, Major!*' he bellowed at the top of his tremendous voice.

*　　*　　*

Wotan's Assault Course was three kilometres of hell dreamed up by all the drill sergeants who had ever lived and some devotee of the Marquis de Sade. A fifty metre crawl up a sheer slope under knee-high barbed wire, with the permanently flowing hosepipes turning the slope into a sea of slippery mud;

a great wall of planks ten metres high which ripped the nails off any trainee who didn't make its top the first time; 'Smoky Sepp's', a dark cavern of a wooden hut filled all the time with choking tear gas, to be entered at the base and left through the hole in the roof; a breath-catching plunge into a chest-deep stream with the instructors tossing thunderflashes in either side of the gasping, straining, crimson-faced trainees; a never-ending kilometre dash across rugged country with thirty kilos of equipment on the back, ending only when one threw one's leathern-lunged, pain-racked body into the damp grass to fire ten rounds of rapid fire into moving targets.

Even then the Butcher had no mercy on them. As they lay there in the wet grass, face downwards gasping frantically for breath, he towered above them and cried cynically: 'Three kilometres in thirty minutes, gentlemen of the Hitler Youth! What do you think Wotan is – a rest-home for fucking gentle-women! Too much five against one, I'll be bound.' He made his meaning clear with an obscene movement of his right hand. 'But by the great whore of Buxtehude, I'll soon stop that kind of piggery! I'll make men of you bunch of slack-assed boy scouts yet. All right you bunch of rooting sows – on yer feet!'

Swaying as if they would collapse, the volunteers crawled to their feet, eyes blank and unseeing, crimson faces running with sweat, huge pearls of perspiration gleaming in their eyebrows.

The Butcher posed in front of them, hands contemptuously on big hips. 'Volunteers,' he declared, 'I've shit 'em! But I've given my solemn promise to Major von Dodenberg that I'll try to make soldiers out of you. I know it's tempting the fates to try. No one in his right mind would think it shitting possible. But the Butcher's got a good heart. *All right!*' he screamed with sudden fury, the veins standing out at his throat, his ugly face flushing, '*at the double! This time we're gonna to do it in*' – he pressed the key of his stop-watch, '*in fifteen!*'

The volunteers staggered like dying men towards the muddy slope.

*   *   *

Major von Dodenburg stood on a sandy hillock, the sea wind ripping at his clothes. 'Comrades,' he lectured the volunteers, already burned a brick-red by the wind and the July sun, 'at ten o'clock and two o'clock, you will see two heights.' The volunteers turned to follow the direction of his outstretched hand.

'On those two heights, small parties of British commandos have established themselves. The commandos are tough, stubborn men who will not surrender. They will fight to the end. How do you deal with them? You winkle them out at the end of the bayonet. The British cannot stand the cold steel. But,' he raised his forefinger warningly. 'They are armed with their standard automatic rifle, accurate at four hundred metres. You wouldn't make it standing up. But still they have to be eradicated. After all the CO will be awarded a fresh piece of tin if you do and that is reason enough, isn't it?' He smiled thinly.

But there was no answering smile from the volunteers. Already the brutalisation process was beginning to have its effect. Their faces remained hard, set in the expression of would-be killers, intent solely on learning their chosen profession to perfection.

'So what do you do? You crawl!' His voice hardened, yet somehow inside he was saddened by what he was having to do to these young innocents in order to turn them into soldiers. 'And to make completely sure that you keep your fool heads down, Sergeants Metzger and Lansch will begin firing from the heights when I give the signal. At exactly fifty centimetres above the ground. So keep your turnips down.' He swung round and waved his hands above his helmeted head.

Metzger and Lansch waved back; they were ready. 'All right,' von Dodenburg commanded, *'down!'*

They dropped in unison into the parched, yellow grass. Hastily von Dodenburg checked the line of young men. Satisfied, he barked: 'Begin crawling – *now*!'

At the same moment, the two NCOs opened up with their mgs. A vicious stream of red and white tracer hissed above the helmeted heads of the young men crawling desperately through the dusty grass towards the heights. Von Dodenburg breathed a sigh of relief. Everything was running smoothly. Two hundred metres, one hundred metres. In a moment the soldiers would be in the dead ground below the mgs. Then as they had been trained they would rise to their feet, bayonets gleaming in the July sun and race towards the Spandaus to finish off their crews with the cold steel of which the Tommies (as was universally known) were so afraid.

Fifty metres! The frantically crawling young men were almost there now. One of the volunteers miscalculated. With a hoarse cry of rage, bayonet gripped in his dirty hands, he sprang to his feet. It was the last move he was ever to make.

Neither Metzger or Lansch hesitated. The vicious red stream of crossfire caught the volunteer in mid-stride. He faltered and screamed shrilly as the slugs ripped his stomach apart.

'Shitty greenback,' said Metzger as he spat drily into the dust at the dead boy's feet.

FIVE

Thus as July 1942 drew to an end Number One Company became the cold-blooded killers that Himmler needed for his new division.

Their days were full of burning sun and tearing sea winds, hoarse bellowed commands and unrelieved strain which had them gasping from lungs that sounded like broken bellows, limbs trembling, days broken only by hastily swallowed meals of disgustingly greasy, cold 'Old Man', reputedly made from the bodies of dead pensioners.

Their nights were little different. It was rare that Metzger and his sadistic NCOs allowed them to sleep more than a couple of hours in a stretch. Thunderflashes tossed through the open windows of their wooden barracks exploded frighteningly under their three-storey high bunks or the sudden alarming chatter of an MG 42, breaking the stillness of the French night, would indicate the commencement of another new scheme to torture their young bodies.

'Righto! Hands off yer cocks and on with yer socks!' the NCOs would scream deafeningly, hammering at the doors with their canes. 'Out of those wanking pits and off with those silken nighties!'

Furiously they would spring, still dazed with sleep, from their beds, tear off their thick woollen nightshirts and stand nakedly at rigid attention. Lips curled contemptuously the NCOs would parade the length of their ranks, barking at them to 'suck in those morbid guts', and 'sock back that turnip, soldier, till it hurts', and making malicious comments about their lack of manhood, pointing their canes derisively at the embarrassed boys, then bellowing: 'Masquerade – we're going dancing, lovely boys! At the double!'

Masquerade entailed changing into fatigues complete with full equipment, before stripping naked at full speed and scrambling furiously into number one uniform, complete with SS dagger and walking out cap. That completed, they would go 'dancing' – hopping up and down the length of the barracks completely naked, absurd and crimson-faced with embarrassment, while the NCOs chivvied them on all sides, striking their bare rumps with canes, crying in voices thickened by years of cheap booze and even cheaper cigars, 'Come on, you bunch of warm wet-tails, get the lead out of your lovely asses! Cos if yer don't, I'll be forced to get out the vaseline in a minute! Move it!' And they would guffaw coarsely.

And more often than not the Vulture, lurking in the shadows outside, would let his suddenly hot eyes feast on their handsome, naked young bodies spread out so appealingly, remembering other places and other young men – the soft, shaven, perfumed flesh of those pliant youngsters with the lisping voices and plucked eyebrows he used to meet in the electric darkness of Berlin's Kudamm.

The ruthless training began to pay dividends. Lean as the volunteers had been at the beginning of their initiation into Wotan's training methods, now they were almost skeletal, their eyes luminous in faces that had been hollowed out into death's heads. They were capable of going all day without food or water, carrying out the murderous training exercises in the lonely coastal countryside as if they had always been used to marching fifty kilometres in five hours with sixty pounds of equipment on their backs.

Major von Dodenburg's pride and confidence in them grew daily. Now, as the mess buzzed with strange rumours of imminent action for the Battalion, and more and more units of the battered Adolf Hitler Bodyguard Division began to appear in the little villages and hamlets which surrounded Dieppe, he started to give Number One Company the final polish that would make it into a worthy member of the Wotan.

It was during one such company-strength field-firing exercise on the great white cliffs beyond the port of Dieppe, when one of the young aeroplane spotters cupped his hands around his mouth and yelled: 'Aircraft to the west! Approaching rapidly!' The company dropped as one, crawling rapidly to any available cover, rifles and mgs already pointing upwards, waiting for the order to fire.

Alarmed, von Dodenburg swung round and focused his binoculars on the dark outline of the strange plane. For a moment he couldn't identify it. Then it sprang into focus within the gleaming circle of glass and he spotted the black and white cross of the *Luftwafle*. It was a Fieseler Storch. He sighed with relief, and lowering his glasses, shouted: 'All right, men, you can get up, it's one of ours!'

The volunteers rose slowly to their feet, dusting the knees of their fatigues, eyeing the black-painted plane curiously as it came lower, savouring the few moments of respite from the gruelling exercise. Von Dodenburg allowed them the break. He, too, was interested in the Storch. For it was obvious, as the pilot circled for a second time at a height of two hundred metres, that he was looking for a place to land.

Finally he lowered his flaps and came zooming in at 150 kilometres an hour to touch down in a perfect three-point landing a hundred metres away. Von Dodenburg stuffed his glasses into their case and hurried across the field towards the plane.

The door opened and a big, broad, well-remembered face beamed out at him on a massive frame that filled the opening. 'Has Sergeant Schulze permission to speak to the Gentleman-Major?' the ex-docker asked cheekily, addressing von Dodenburg in the manner once used by NCOs speaking to officers in the Old Army. Behind him someone tried to push past him and he jerked his elbow backwards in irritation. 'Get on my back, you crippled little monkey-turd! Can't you hear I'm talking to the CO.'

'*Schulze!*' von Dodenburg exclaimed, pushing back his helmet from his sweating brow in surprise, 'what in three devils' name are you doing here?'

'Courtesy of the *Reichsheini*, sir,' Schulze explained easily, lowering his eyes modestly. 'This is his personal Storch.'

'What? *Himmler?*' von Dodenburg stuttered, 'His ... his ... plane?'

'That's right, sir,' Matz answered, pushing beneath Schulze's big arm, his wizened face one huge grin, a pile of parcels in his arms. 'And we bring gifts to the Company – firewater and cancer sticks – for the brave boys of the Wotan. I quote the *Reichsheini's* own words.'

'But you're supposed to be in hospital in Berlin.'

Schulze did not reply. Instead he dropped to the grass and reached out a plaster-clad hand to Matz. 'All right, you little cripple, come on down.' He helped the Corporal to the ground. 'All right,' he ordered grandly, poking his big head into the cockpit to the pilot. 'You can take her away now, my man. And please convey my respects to the Reichsführer when you return to Berlin. Off you go!'

Von Dodenburg waited till the roar had died away. Then he said: 'Well you two rogues, I can't deny I'm glad to see your ugly mugs again. I can use good NCOs in due course. But what the devil am I to do with you for the time being – you're hardly in a fit state for combat at the moment, are you?'

Schulze scowled. 'Even with no hands, sir, I'm better than that lot of greenbeaks over there. Still got the eggshell behind their spoons by the look of them! Heaven, arse and twine, Matzi, what is the Armed SS coming to? Look at them. I bet that lot of milk-toasts couldn't even get themselves a piece of nooky in a knocking-shop!'

Von Dodenburg laughed and shook his head, 'I don't know Schulze, you're as incorrigible as ever. But what am I going to do with the pair of you?'

He stood the company down and they sprawled out happily

on the turf, savouring the hot July sun while von Dodenburg pondered the problem, smoking one of the 'cancer-sticks' sent personally by the *Reichsheini*.

'You said just a minute ago that they,' he indicated the teenaged volunteers all around, 'that they couldn't even get themselves a piece of nooky in a knocking-shop. By that, I presume you mean they are too innocent to buy themselves a woman of no virtue in a house of ill-fame?'

Schulze looked at Matz. 'Did you hear all those big words, Matzi? I think the CO is trying to pull our pissers – ever so gently but definitely. That's what I think.'

Von Dodenburg laughed. 'All right, Schulze. Now listen. This weekend we stand down for forty-eight hours on the CO's orders. So what will those milk-toasts, as you call them, do? I'll tell you, Schulze – they'll head for the brothels of Rouen and Dieppe as quickly as their feet will take them, clutching their fifty francs in their hot sticky hands. They might be young, but they are still very healthy male animals and they've all heard about French women in bed.'

'I didn't think they liked girls much,' Matz said, taking a quick sip from one of Himmler's presentation flatmen.

The Major ignored him. 'So Schulze and Matz, you're the self-confessed experts on all things female.'

'I've had me moments,' Schulze admitted modestly.

'Good. Then I've got a job for you. From now onwards you're the Company's official VD patrol. You'll check every other ranks' brothel in Dieppe out and put it out-of-bounds to Number One Company if you find a girl in it without her yellow card stamped right up to date by the local French police doctors. I'm not having any of my men going down with disease now.' He poked a finger at them. 'And I shall make you two personally responsible if we get one single case of VD this week.'

'Holy straw sack!' Schulze exclaimed. 'What do you say to that Matzi? Look how low you've gone and dragged me now.

A shitty pox-cop indeed!'

Five minutes later, however, he had recovered sufficiently from the shock of his new assignment to ask Major von Dodenburg a question that took the smile off his handsome young face and replaced it with a look of taut foreboding. 'But sir, what in hell's name is the Battalion doing in this God-forsaken Frog hole? That's what I would like to know – why are we in Dieppe?'

'Well, Schulze,' von Dodenburg replied slowly. 'I'd like to know the answer to that question myself.'

SIX

'*Meine Herren*,' announced General Hase, the Commander of the 15th Army, formally, 'his Excellency, Field Marshal von Rundstedt!'

The assembled officers of the First SS Division under the command of the barrel-chested Divisional Commander, ex-tank sergeant and Munich Party bully boy Sepp Dietrich, snapped to attention. For even the officers of the SS's premier division who had normally little respect for the field-greys of the Wehrmacht, admired the planning genius of Germany's foremost soldier.

An incredibly old and wrinkled officer appeared through the door of the operations room, huddled, despite the July heat, in a thick greatcoat with a fur-trimmed collar.

Weakly von Rundstedt raised his baton to acknowledge their greeting. 'You may be seated, gentlemen,' he said slowly, in a voice made hoarse by the French cognac to which he was addicted.

The dignified old man who commanded Germany's destiny in the West waited patiently till the assembled officers had taken their places, then he tottered slowly over to the great map which covered one wall of the ops room.

'Gentlemen of the Bodyguard Division,' he began, 'we can expect the Tommies to attempt a major landing in the Dieppe area in the next week or so.'

There was an excited buzz of chatter and von Rundstedt smiled thinly, pleased with the effect of his words.

'We have it on good authority from our V-men* in Southern England that the Tommies are massing troops for the

* *Vertrauensmann*, man-of-trust, ie agent. (Transl.)

43

attempt. In the Führer's opinion, Churchill is being forced into making the attempt by pressure from the Bolsheviks and the Americans.' He coughed throatily. The bemedalled chief aide, who knew the signal well, hurried across the room with the unlabelled bottle. 'Your cough medicine, your Excellency,' he said and poured out a generous measure.

'Thank you, Heinz. I must have caught a cold on the way here.' He took a deep drink of the cognac, while von Dodenburg threw the Vulture a significant glance.

But the CO's cold blue eyes were fixed on the ancient Field Marshal, tensed for his next words, obviously hoping that Wotan would be involved in whatever action would come so that he might achieve an even higher rank, his sole ambition in life.

'Excuse me, gentlemen,' von Rundstedt continued, ignoring the knowing smirk on Sepp Dietrich's broad face. He tapped

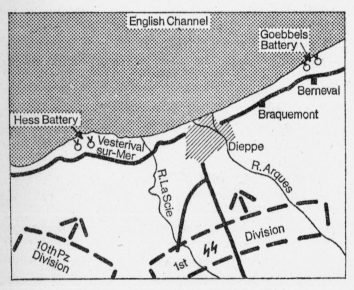

German positions – Dieppe, July 1942

44

the big map. 'Dieppe, the Tommies' target. Now I am sure that the gentlemen of the SS can guess what the Tommies will attempt to do when they land.'

The ancient Field Marshal paused, as if daring any one of the black-clad officers present to take the initiative. But Sepp Dietrich, loud-mouthed and as aggressive as he usually was, dared not do that in the presence of Germany's foremost strategist.

'No,' Rundstedt queried softly, a cynical expression in his faded eyes. 'Then I shall tell you. The Tommies are notoriously wooden and unoriginal in their strategy and tactics. It comes from their rigid class structure no doubt. They tell me that their Army, as amateur as it is, still drills as it did in the days of the Great Frederick.'* He allowed himself a faint smile. 'No matter. It makes them easier meat for us, I suppose. So, what will they do? As you know Dieppe lies in the two kilometre-wide gap at the mouth of River D'Arques. At both ends of that gap there are the formidable headlines – here and here – which dominate the whole area of Dieppe beach – the obvious landing site for our thick-headed Tommies. And of course the Tommies will land there because they will think the old squareheads, as they call us, will not be foolish enough to make a frontal attack on a beach which is so obviously defensible.'

Von Dodenburg stared, open-mouthed. The ancient Field Marshal made his statements with the certainty of a clairvoyant.

'Now what dangers face our Tommy friends apart from the fortified promenade at Dieppe? The twin batteries here and here. The Goebbels Battery at Berneval, named after our beloved Ministry of Propaganda Josef Goebbels and the Hess Battery, here, at Vesterival-sur-mer. Called after someone who shall remain nameless.'

* ie Frederick the Great of Prussia, who ruled in the latter half of the 18th century. (Transl.)

45

Dietrich flushed, while the Field Marshal smiled innocently at him. The Battery was, of course, named after the traitor Rudolf Hess who had betrayed the Führer and the Party by flying to England months before. As usual the Field Marshal was trying to needle the Armed SS, a formation which he passionately hated. Sepp Dietrich swore he'd pay the old senile bastard back one day. Apparently oblivious to his embarrassment, von Rundstedt continued: 'Now these two batteries have specific tasks, as you probably know, if the Tommies land. At the command *Sperrfeuer Dieppe*,* the six 15cm guns of Hess will lay a barrage down in front of Dieppe at a range of eight thousand metres, firing an initial six rounds per gun. Goebbels in the meantime would concentrate on any naval forces further out to sea. So what will the Tommies try to do? They will attempt to knock out those two batteries before they attack in force. What do we conclude from that, gentlemen of the SS? We conclude, that an attack on the two batteries will be the signal for an all out enemy landing within – say – the next hour. Do you follow me?'

The SS officers in their immaculate black uniforms squirmed in embarrassment in their seats; the venerable Field Marshal was treating them like a bunch of school kids, instead of combat-experienced leaders of the premier SS division. Awkwardly they mumbled that they had understood.

'Good, good, gentlemen,' von Rundstedt's face cracked into a wintery smile. 'The Tommies will attack Hess, which is one kilometre inland, by one of two possible beaches – here – near Quiberville and – here – directly in front of the Battery, where there are two gullies, a fault in the cliff.' He shrugged. 'It could be that they will use both beaches. The Tommy generals have little understanding of the principle of concentration in war. No matter. East of Dieppe at Berneval, which comes into the Bodyguard's divisional area, the Tommies similarly have

* A difficult phrase to translate. Literally 'interdiction fire-Dieppe'. (Transl.)

two small beaches available for their assault on Goebbels. Now,' von Rundstedt raised his voice, 'I am prepared to lose Hess. Indeed, I have ordered the commander of the Tenth Panzer Division not to make any great defence of the Battery.'

There was a little gasp of surprise from the SS officers. Von Rundstedt beamed; it was the reaction he had expected from the SS with its stupid policy of never giving up ground, even if by doing so they could achieve great tactical advantage. 'Yes,' he said, reaching out a claw of a hand flecked with a mass of liver spots. 'Like a spider tempting a fly, I want to draw them into my web. I and the Führer want them to land. To land *in force* and be slaughtered in their thousands. It will be a tremendous boast for our prestige here in France and it might even force the Ivans to sue for peace when they see that the Western Allies cannot help them. But I cannot afford to lose Goebbels. The poison dwarf,' he used the Army's contemptuous name for the club-footed, bitter-tongued Minister of Propaganda, 'must remain firmly in German hands. Naturally the Tommies will use their Navy to cover the landings, and those warships will be the only really effective artillery that the Tommies will be able to bring to bear on our positions. Indeed their fire could effectively seal off Dieppe and prevent our reinforcements from moving into the place once the Tommies have landed. So we can afford to lose Hess. We *want* them to land. But we cannot afford to lose Goebbels, because its guns will destroy any attempt by the Royal Navy to stop us slaughtering those troops once they have landed. Now this is where the Bodyguard comes in, gentlemen –'

'Your Excellency.' Sepp Dietrich sprang to his big feet, barrel-chest thrown out proudly, cleft-chin pushed forward aggressively and bellowed, 'Beg to report, Field Marshal, that the Field Marshal can depend upon the Bodyguard to the death!'

Von Rundstedt did not speak while he studied the ex-Party bullyboy as if he were a particularly interesting form of beetle

47

that had just crawled out of the woodwork. 'What a pleasant thought,' he breathed at last, as if the thought of the SS, the 'black scum', as he called them privately, lying dead on Dieppe cliffs gave him some pleasure. 'To the death.'

Sepp Dietrich flushed and dropped back into his seat.

Von Rundstedt looked down at him. 'General, at present your division is composed of what we used to call in the Imperial Army – Christmas Tree soldiers.'

There was an angry murmur from the SS officers.

Von Rundstedt swept on. 'Due to your losses in Russia, your ranks have been filled out by too many raw recruits who have never been in action. I admit they will die bravely if called upon to do so. But if I may be so bold as to lecture the gentlemen of the SS – wars are won by live soldiers, not dead ones. Besides any large scale move by the Bodyguard might well alarm the Tommies on the day, might frighten them off before the trap has closed upon them.' He licked his colourless lips, as if he were considering whether he should cough and alert the attentive Heinz with the cognac. 'However, one of your battalions, General Dietrich, I have been informed, is up to full strength and relatively well trained. It is also located, tactically speaking, in an ideal spot at Braquemont between the Goebbels Battery and Dieppe. It's your First Battalion – the Wotan.'

The Vulture started when he heard the name of his battalion, but unlike Dietrich he knew his Field Marshal Gerd von Rundstedt. Casually he rose to his feet, thrust his monocle in his right eye, and barked in his rasping Prussian voice, 'Your Excellency, one cold fart from my kitchen bulls would suffice to blow the Tommies right back across the Channel.'

Von Rundstedt smiled carefully. He recognised the coarseness of the Regular Army cavalryman and knew instinctively he was speaking to his own kind. 'You are very confident, Colonel.'

The Vulture did not rise to the compliment. Instead, he

snapped: 'Your orders for my Battalion, Your Excellency?'

Again von Rundstedt smiled, showing his large, too white false teeth. He liked the bandy-legged little SS Colonel with his baggy breeches and monstrous beak of a nose. 'It is not customary for a Field Marshal of the German Army to direct the activities of a single battalion, Colonel, although in these days of change who knows to what depths a German Field Marshal might have to sink.'

The Vulture shared the Field Marshal's smile, while two seats away Sepp Dietrich glowered with suppressed anger. 'In this case, however, it is vital to the success of the whole operation that the Goebbels Battery should be held. You, my dear Colonel, will remain at Braquemont until the Tommies actually start landing at the beaches next to the Goebbels.'

'Then, Your Excellency?'

'Then you will march your battalion down the road to the Battery as if the devil himself were after you!'

'*March?*' the Vulture queried.

'Yes, *march.* I am not going to risk your vehicles attracting the unwelcome attention of the RAF which undoubtedly will be over the battlefield at the time, and being knocked out before you ever reach the Battery. You fellows who have been fighting in Russia over this last year simply do not realise the might of the RAF. Fat Hermann* is powerless against them. Hence, my dear Colonel, your men will leave their armour behind at Braquemont and march to battle when the time comes. From this day onwards you will practise marching those five kilometres to the Battery as if your very life depends upon it.' He raised his hand and stared down at the Vulture, his eyes icy.

Von Dodenburg looked at the wrinkled old man and shivered involuntarily. The words were not a warning; they were a naked threat.

* ie the gross Marshal of the German Air Force, Hermann Goering. (Transl.)

SEVEN

'May I address you, Sergeant?' the young SS soldier, with the anxious eyes and fringe of white-blond hair which kept falling over his forehead, shouted at Schulze above the blare of the *bal musette* music which rocked Dieppe's *Cafe de la belle Alliance*.

'Why not?' Schulze said generously, eyeing the floor crowded with giggling drunken whores, happy, sweating soldiers and men of the *Kriegsmarine*.

'Are you familiar with this place?' the boy shouted.

'I am,' Schulze answered, not taking his eyes off the floor, watching intently for any man from the First Company, 'it's Rosi-Rosi's knocking shop.'

'Good. That's why I'm here.'

Both Matz and Schulze swung round as one and stared at him. 'Are you in the First Company?' Matz demanded, fully conscious of von Dodenburg's threat to have them sent back to *la Charité* and Sister Klara if one single man of his Hitler Youth volunteers caught a dose.

The boy shook his blond head. 'No, the Third.'

They breathed out a sigh of relief. 'Then that's all right. Go on, soldier, what do you want?'

'A woman,' the boy answered baldly.

'You've come to the right place, lad,' Matz said, 'Rosi-Rosi is right on target if you want to get rid of your dirty water.'

The boy flushed with embarrassment. 'I know, Corporal. But you see I want a special woman.'

Schulze looked at him curiously. 'What do you fancy – one with two of 'em? Or with it tucked in neatly under her armpit?' He grinned suddenly at the thought. 'Matzi, imagine what it would be like if they had 'em there? Yer wouldn't even have to take yer dice-beakers off to get a bit.' He made an obscene gesture with his elbow to illustrate what he meant.

'I can't get mine off as it is,' the boy said, 'after today's five kilometres in fifteen minutes. My feet are like raw meat.'

'Tough tittie,' Matz said unfeelingly. 'But get on with it, lad, what kind of special piece do you want?'

'Well, it's hard to explain – but she's got to be nice as well as screwable. I mean I'd like to be able to talk to her –'

'*Afterwards?*' Matz queried.

'Yes, afterwards of course,' the boy agreed.

Schulze shook his head. 'Jesus H. Christ, Matzi,' he exclaimed, 'what's the Army coming to! This wet-tail here wants to *talk* to a piece. Great crap on the Christmas Tree, you don't pay 'em to talk, lad, you pay 'em to lie on their backs with their pearly gates open!'

'Give him a chance, Schulze,' Matz protested. 'He's a nice boy. He probably drinks his nigger sweat with his little pinkie stuck out like this.'

'I'd like somebody I could live with a bit while we're in France,' the boy persisted.

'What about my old woman?' Matz volunteered with a scowl. 'You can have her, if you like – and I'll throw in twenty marks.'

The boy smiled. 'No, she's got to be French.'

'Hey,' Schulze snapped. The big frizzy-haired brunette behind the bar swung round.

'What you want?' she called in her fluent, ungrammatical German.

'You, Rosi-Rosi.'

She put down the glass she was cleaning. 'I come, Sergeant Schulze,' she answered.

'Yeah, *you* might,' Matz chortled, 'but Sergeant Schulze *don't*!'

'Currant-crapper!' Schulze cursed, but only half-heartedly;

51

his attention was directed on the brunette brothel-owner, who had gained her nickname Rosi-Rosi from the rouged nipples of her huge breasts which had a habit of popping out of her low-cut silk dress at odd moments. 'Shit on the shingle,' he breathed admiringly, 'I'd like to get my choppers into them. And look at that ass on her, Matzi – like a ten dollar mare!'

Rosi-Rosi stopped in front of their table, the tops of her breasts trembling like jellies. 'Yes,' she demanded, 'what you got in mind, Sergeant?'

'It's not in my mind,' Schulze leered up at her, 'it's in my britches.'

'Then keep the filthy thing there,' Rosi-Rosi said without rancour.

'Come?'

'If only he could!' Matz exclaimed.

Schulze ignored him. 'It's this lad here, Rosi-Rosi. He's just had an unhappy love affair.'

'Yes?' Rosi-Rosi leaned forward curiously, giving Schulze a panoramic view of her magnificent breasts and their rouged nipples.

'Sure. He broke his right hand!' Schulze laughed out loud at his own humour.

'*Sale con!*' the Madame cursed in her own language, but there was a twinkle in her bright blue eyes all the same. Nor did she object when Schulze put his plastered paw experimentally on her dimpled plump knee.

'But seriously, Rosi-Rosi, this lad here has decided to give up the old five against one and take up with girls – you know, boys in skirts? But she's got to be different – she's got to be someone he can talk to.' He winked hugely. 'He's a bit funny that way.'

'Germans,' Rosi-Rosi sighed. She swung round, her breasts quivering. 'Jo-Jo,' she said to the cross-eyed bartender with a

Galoise glued to his bottom lip. 'He wants a cunt he can talk to.'

Jo-Jo nodded. He dived into the heaving, sweating throng and emerged a moment later with a fat girl with a moon face who looked like two sacks of potatoes tied together by the belt that disappeared into the soft pillow of her massive stomach.

'Jeanne,' Rosi-Rosi announced and stroked the enormous girl's hair which looked as if it had been cropped by a cross-eyed barber.

'Christ,' Schulze exclaimed, 'Jeanne d'Arc!'

But the boy seemed well enough satisfied. A few moments later he was deep in an excited conversation with the girl, replete with many hand gestures and *'oui-ouis'*.

Schulze turned his attention to Rosi-Rosi. 'You and me could make beautiful music together, *cherie*,' he said, putting his big hand around her well-corsetted waist and drawing her massive bosom close to his face.

'Watch it, Schulze,' Matz said urgently, 'she'll poke yer right eye out with her tit if you're not careful.'

'You want jig-jig?' Rosi-Rosi said, seemingly oblivious to Schulze's big plastered paw already fumbling beneath her skirt.

'Want it?' Schulze exclaimed energetically. 'If I had to get up now, Rosi-Rosi, there wouldn't be a glass left on this table, and I'm not shitting you!'

Rosi-Rosi laughed and her breasts quivered delightfully. Schulze grew bolder. He thrust his paw right up between her legs. Rosi-Rosi jumped. 'It is very hard – and hot!'

'It's not the only thing either,' Schulze said darkly. 'Now if you and me could only –'

But Schulze was not fated to enjoy Rosi-Rosi's delectable charms that night. For suddenly the thick big felt blackout curtain which covered the cafe's door was flung back to admit the massive frame of the Butcher and a group of his cronies, all flushed and obviously deep in their cups. He spotted

Schulze and the woman at once and bawled drunkenly so that everyone could hear: 'Get yer paws off'n him, Rosi-Rosi! That particular fart-cannon, masquerading as an NCO, is First Company's pox-cop. You never know that yer can catch from even touching him.' He opened his big arms in welcome. 'Come on over to Pappa, where you're nice and snug and safe.'

Rosi-Rosi released herself from Schulze's grip and pushed her way through the laughing throng towards the big Sergeant-Major, who clutched her round the waist and staggered off with her to the nearest table, which he cleared by the simple expedient of kicking the nearest soldier over the back of his chair.

'Perverted banana-sucker!' Schulze growled morosely. 'If I only had his missus under me tonight, I'd give her a right old rattle for that, I would!'*

'Rank hath its privileges,' Matz said in sympathy. 'And besides you've got to admit – there's plenty of other talent around.'

'Hm,' Schulze grunted and sank into a sullen silence, glowering at the whores in their thin flowered dresses, and the sweating servicemen, their big knees jammed deep into the women's crotches as they swept round in the tango.

But Schulze wasn't allowed to wallow for long in his despair or his unspoken plans for taking some terrible revenge on the Butcher.

'Hey Schulze,' Matz broke into his reverie, 'there's one of ours and look at that pig he's dancing with. If anybody's got a full house, she has.'

Schulze looked at the First Company soldier tangoing with a whore who could have been his mother, her long tongue stuck in his ear with professional concupiscence, breathing hard with pretended passion. Her chin was covered with red sores.

'Well, come on, you sewer stomach. Don't sit there like a

* For further details of this episode, see *SS Panzer Battalion*.

54

spare prick at a wedding. That wet-tail's probably got stiff of the ear already the way she's got her spotty tongue stuck in it.'

The two of them shoved back their chairs and barged their way through the crowd, bowling protesting soldiers and whores to both sides.

Schulze dropped his big hand on the whore's thin shoulder. 'Yer yellow card,' he demanded.

'Piss off!' she said, still dancing.

'Hey sergeant,' protested the soldier, 'don't give me a hard time. I'm only here for the dancing. The way they marched us to the Goebbels yesterday, I haven't even got the strength to get it up.'

But Schulze was still in a bad mood. 'The CO said I've got to check their shitty yellow cards to see that they don't start spreading any little Frenchie souvenirs around once they take off their drawers. All right, *cherie*, let's have the card.'

'Piss off!' the whore repeated over her shoulder. She pressed her belly deeper into the soldier's. 'Come on, shuffle 'em, soldier.'

'I'm not telling you another time –' Schulze began, just as a fat *Obermaat* of the Navy bumped into his back and nearly knocked him off his feet.

He spun round angrily. 'Are you blind, you perverted naval banana-sucker?' he cried.

'What yer standing in the middle of the shitty floor for then?' snarled the *Obermaat*. 'Stupid SS sod – got to be told to come out of the rain some of 'em!'

'You're looking for a knuckle-sandwich,' Schulze said threateningly, bringing up his plastered fist.

The *Obermaat* relinquished his hold on his partner. 'You talking to me, soldier?'

'Who do you think – the shitting Big Lion* himself?'

* The title given by his submariners to the head of the Submarine Service, Admiral Doenitz. (Transl.)

55

'Admiral Doenitz, to you, you nasty poisonous garden-dwarf.'

Schulze flushed. 'You're gonna get a mouthful of knuckles if you're not careful, you fat fart-cannon!'

'Hey, what gives here?' Rosi-Rosi burst through the circle around the little group. 'We're here for jig-jig, not for box-box.'

'I told him,' protested the First Company boy earnestly, 'that I only want to dance with the whore. After yesterday's march to Berneval –'

Matz jabbed his elbow into the boy's stomach and his words ended in a sudden gasp as he doubled up. At the same moment the fat *Obermaat* launched a tremendous punch at Schulze. The big NCO ducked just in time. Unable to stop, the *Obermaat* staggered into Rosi-Rosi. Caught by surprise, she shrieked with such force that her red-tipped breasts popped out of the confines of her silken dress.

But even that tremendous display of naked flesh could not stop the fight which was spreading with spectacular speed. Bottles flew through the air. Glasses crunched underfoot. Here and there whores crawled under overturned tables. The three-man band faded away with one last gasp of a dying accordion.

A beer mug hit Schulze on the back of his big head. He staggered forward dizzily. Through the bloody haze he caught a glimpse of the Butcher's ugly face grinning at him. 'Serves you shitting well right,' the Sergeant-Major growled and shoved him back into the fighting, screaming, howling throng with the toe of his boot.

'Arsehole!' Schulze growled, then shaking his head like a bull brushing away a swarm of tormenting flies, went to work on the sailors all around.

From outside there came the howl of a military police truck.

'The chain dogs!' Matz gasped, grabbing Schulze's arm.

'Let me go! I'll slaughter the bastards, every single one of the currant crappers!'

'Come on,' Matz cried desperately. 'You don't want to go back to the Charité do you, you stupid horned-ox? This way – through the window of the piss corner.'

Swiftly the two of them carved a path through the brawling mob and disappeared into the latrine, one second before the military police rushed in through the door, their rubber clubs at the ready.

* * *

Thirty minutes later the MPs had dragged the last struggling servicemen out and the Lieutenant in charge had signed the chit which Jo-Jo had handed him, to certify that the German Town Commandant would be responsible for all damage caused by the brawlers. Now Rosi-Rosi stood there in the empty cafe, surveying the wreckage and massaging her left breast, as if she were kneading bread. But her mind was not on the mess of broken furniture and smashed bottles. It was on the two boys' strange words. Why had both of them complained about their feet? And what were the Wotan boche doing marching to Goebbels – the battery located at Berneval – when they had plenty of transport? It might mean something and then again it might mean nothing. Still one couldn't be too careful. In the end she made up her mind. 'Jo-Jo,' she called.

'Yes, Rosi-Rosi,' her small lover replied, the cigarette still stuck to his thick wet bottom lip.

'That Boche Sergeant-Major wants to stick his meat into me in thirty minutes at his quarters.'

Jo-Jo nodded, bored. 'So?'

'I haven't got time. You'll have to go, Jo-Jo.'

'Where?'

'To see the Englishman. I want you to tell him this . . .'

EIGHT

'Cor ferk a duck,' Colonel, the Laird of Abernockie and Dearth groaned in pure Cockney and tugged at his over-long kilt to keep the keen sea wind from blowing it up. 'It's parky about the goolies in these sodding things, Freddy!'

Major the Hon Freddy Rory-Brick, known behind his back to the men of Number Seven Commando as red prick, took his gaze off the green, swaying mass of the Channel, 'Well, you don't weally need to wear one, sir.' Languidly he screwed his monocle tighter in his eye and looked down at the tiny, red-haired figure of his CO in his tam o'shanter and drooping Abernockie kilt. 'Do you, now?'

'What do you mean, you long streak of Scots Guard piss! I'm the Laird, ain't I. The lads expect it from me. Besides, Freddy, when yer a CO like me you have to keep up with the Joneses. If Lovat of the Fourth Commando can wear civvie bags and have his personal piper, and Jock Churchill of the Third can go into action with that great ruddy sword of his, I've got to have this bleeding tweed skirt.' He swept his hands across the great white V of the Eureka landing craft speeding towards the chalk cliffs. 'My gillies and gamekeepers like me to keep up the old traditions. They're just as toffee-nosed as you are, Freddy.'

'Toffee-nosed, sir!' the Scots Guard Major exclaimed. 'Weally, Colonel, you do use the most extwaordinary ex-pwessions!'

The Laird gave the other man one of the sly grins which had gained him the nickname of 'Foxy Fergus' in the days when he had been a barrow boy in the Tottenham Court Road before, to his complete surprise, a long forgotten great uncle, the Laird of Abernockie and Dearth, had died and he had been informed he owned 'half o' ruddy northern Scotland'. 'All right, Freddy,' he said. 'Screw in that window-pane firmly, and finger out. Here they come! Start timing 'em!'

As the first Eureka crunched into the shingle one hundred feet below, the big Major pressed down the catch of his stop-watch. The last rehearsal had begun.

The ramp slapped the wet pebbles. Swiftly, expertly, the men of Number 7 Commando doubled to left and right, pelting up the beach towards the base of the cliffs. They dropped simultaneously, Tommy guns at the ready, forming a defensive screen round the two rocket launchers.

'Stand back, Freddy!' the Laird rapped.

Not a moment too soon. There was a soft belch as the men below fired the grapnel launchers. Two swift puffs of white smoke. From their centres two great gleaming grapnels burst into the open, heading for the top of the cliff. Behind them sneaked a wildly quivering 100-foot length of stout rope. The first hook hit the chalk metallicly. A second later the other grapnel gripped fast.

'Two minutes, sir,' Freddy announced.

'Sodding spot on!' the Laird exclaimed, feeling his blood already beginning to run faster with a sense of rising excitement.

Two burly sergeants grasped the ropes. Without a second's hesitation they started to scramble upwards, while a Tommy-gunner sprayed the top of the cliff with blank ammunition. Another pair of commandos grasped the rope. Now more and more Eurekas were hitting the beach. The air seemed full of flying grapnels.

'Bash on, lads!' the Laird cried, his kilt flying up about his spindly shanks unnoticed now.

The first crimson faces appeared above the edge of the cliff.

'Five minutes!' rapped Freddy.

Eyes wild and staring, chests heaving with the effort, the

commandos unslung their weapons. Crouched low, they dashed for the first line of apron wire. On the heights above Southsea's Home Guard, the enemy opened fire with blank slugs.

A corporal flung himself at the wire at full-tilt, arms out-stretched. He screamed shrilly as the wire bit into his body. But already the second man was running up his impaled body and dropping over the other side. More and more of the commandos followed him across the human bridge.

'That's it, lads!' the Laird screamed. 'Give 'em sodding hell! Mix it!' His eyes gleamed excitedly; the weeks of remorseless training were paying off.

'Eight minutes!' Freddy cried.

His comrades hauled the bloody human bridge across the wire. Now they broke up into little groups of four and five, each under the command of an officer or NCO. Swiftly they doubled to their allotted positions facing the seven simulated mg pits which they knew from Intelligence surrounded the Battery.

The Laird raised his Very pistol.

'Ten minutes,' Freddy announced, even his voice excited now. The Laird pressed the trigger. Once. Twice. The two bright red flares hushed into the English sky.

It was the signal. In perfect unison, the commandos opened up with their automatics. The morning was full of the crazy chatter of blank. Training Mills bombs sailed through the air like black rain. In the same instant, one man dashed forward from each group, zig-zagging violently like rugby internationals going in for a try, firing from the hip as they did so.

'Here come the Wangers!' Freddy cried.

The mg posts taken, the handful of US Rangers attached to the Commando doubled forward through the gap in the line, lugging their ten-foot-long Bangalore torpedoes with them.

'Come on, Yanks. Move them all-American legs of yourn!' the Laird screamed excitedly.

Expertly the Americans slithered through the grass in one wild dive and thrust their Bangalores beneath the triple line of apron wire directly in front of the wooden mock-up of the Battery.

For a moment nothing happened. Then there was a violet flash of cordite and wire flew everywhere.

'Twelve minutes, sir!'

The smoke was split by scarlet muzzle flashes. Gradually the firing began to die away. The rapid snap and crackle of small arms became the odd dry crack. Abruptly a green flare sailed out of the smoke and hung there in the sky, tinging everything below it an eerie, sickly hue.

'The signal!' the Laird exclaimed excitedly. 'How long Freddy? Well, come on, old cock – how long?'

Freddy pressed the stop. 'Exactly sixteen minutes and wather more than thirty seconds!'

The Laird of Abernockie and Dearth beamed up at the tall elegant guardsman. 'Ain't yer window pane steamed up with excitement, Freddy?' he cried. 'We did it – right on time!'

'Yes, it was weally wather impwessive, sir.' The Laird, now in high good humour, gave him a soft raspberry.

*   *   *

The Laird had just finished inspecting his men still sprawled out on the cropped turf, chests heaving, sweat-glazed faces crimson, when the DR roared in from the main Southsea–Havant road. At sixty he bumped across the uneven ground, scattering the elderly Home Guards, bouncing up and down in his saddle.

'Bet his knackers hurt tonight, Freddy!' the Laird said, watching his exhibitionist progress with interest.

'Wonder what's the hurry, sir?'

'Search me. Perhaps Winnie wants me to make me maiden speech in 'Ouse.'

With an impressive screech of protesting rubber, the

leather-jerkined DR braked. He thrust up his goggles and snapped to attention when he recognised the strange little officer's badges-of-rank. 'Colonel, the Laird of –'

'All right, put a plug in it, mate,' interrupted the CO of the Commando, 'we don't want to be all day. What yer got for me, son?'

A little bewildered by the Cockney accent coming from what was supposedly a Scottish lord, the DR opened his pouch and took out a sealed buff envelope. 'Your eyes only, sir. From Combined Ops HQ,' he barked.

'Don't rupture yersen,' the Laird said sourly. Taking the envelope, he walked to one side and taking the skean dhu from his sock, slit it open.

He read it slowly, as if he were having difficulty in under-standing its contents, his grey face growing grimmer by the second.

A few yards away the Home Guards were jingling their mess tins hopefully, for a 'pint of real sergeant-major's tea'. Freddy knew it was his responsibility. But the look on his CO's face told him that it was not the right time to order a tea-break.

'Anything the matter, sir?' he asked finally.

'Come over her, Freddy,' the Laird replied.

'Sir.'

'Freddy, I can't let you read this dispatch. It's from Richmond Terrace – Intelligence – and for my peepers only. But I'll be buggered if they can stop me telling you roughly what's in it.'

'Sir?'

The Laird lowered his voice. 'Freddy, Intelligence reports that a Jerry battalion is practising speed marches up the road to Berneval,' he announced gloomily.

'So?'

'So, you big streak of piss, doesn't it tie in with the ruddy fact that it's exactly thirty-nine days since we abandoned

Operation Butter* and that since then every sodding pub from Pompey to Plymouth has been full of squaddies and matelots spilling their guts to anybody who'd buy 'em a pint! You can bet yer bottom dollar that the Jerries have got on to us.' He stared gloomily out at the heaving green, white-capped sea. 'Freddy, I think the Jerries know we're coming.'

The Guardsman stared down at him aghast. In spite of his ludicrous lower class accent and even more ludicrous attempt to ape an upper class Scottish lord, Freddy knew that Fergus MacDonald was no fool. Since he'd formed his own commando from his tenants and a handful of volunteers from the Glasgow slums in early 1941, the Colonel had learned faster than many a professional officer. He had done well at Vaagso and even better at St Nazaire, winning the MC at the first and the DSO at the second. The CO's long crafty nose that had once given him his nickname of 'Foxy Fergus' could smell trouble a mile away, and where many a professional officer simply bashed on and took his knocks, the CO preferred to 'use the back door', as he was fond of explaining at training sessions.

'I don't know. I can't put me finger on it, as the actress said to the bishop,' the Laird said sombrely. 'All the same, I can feel it in my bones – they know!'

'Pon my soul,' Freddy exclaimed. 'But sir, they wouldn't let us walk into a twap, would they?'

The CO didn't answer. Instead he said, 'Freddy, you take charge here.'

'What?'

'Yes, I'm off.' He swung round and shouted at the DR. 'Hey, you.'

'Sir?'

'Bring that bike of yours over here at the double!'

The DR thrust down his goggles and rumbled the heavy

* The first raid on Dieppe cancelled in early July when the attack force was already on board ship. (Transl.)

63

motorbike across the rough ground towards him. The Colonel flung his leg over the pillion, carelessly revealing that in true Scots fashion, he wasn't wearing underpants. 'All right, let her rip!'

'Yessir!' The bike roared into noisy life. The diminutive Colonel took a firmer grip of the DR's waist and tensed expectantly.

'But where are you orff to, sir?' the Hon Freddy Rory-Brick demanded, his celebrated calm vanished for once.

'To the Big Smoke,' yelled the Laird of Abernockie and Dearth, the wind snatching at his words as the bike tore away, 'I'm gonnna have a word with his Lordship...'

'Oh, Chwist!' Freddy cursed and clutched his forehead.

NINE

The Commando Colonel was not the only officer concerned that day. As midday approached on that Sunday, 16th August 1942, Colonel Geier and Major von Dodenberg cantered together down the straight road from Braquemont to Berneval on their hired horses. To any watching peasant preparing to dig into his Sunday rabbit, they looked like a score of other Boche officers they had seen riding down the same road on Sunday afternoons these last two years – immaculate, lordly, aloof, part of a world that had nothing to do with their own lowly existence.

But the two SS officers were not out riding for pleasure; they were on duty. As the Vulture had rasped to von Dodenburg when he had ordered the latter to hire the horses: 'Von Rundstedt is a damn clever strategist, von Dodenburg. But the old fart has never heard a shot fired in anger since 1918. He doesn't know that on the battlefield everything doesn't work out so smoothly as one of his big charts at St Germain.'* Thus the two of them cantered easily down the road, their horses' rumps gleaming with sweat, keen eyes searching the countryside on both sides for obstacles, possible sources of trouble, difficulties.

'Assuming the Tommies will land before dawn,' the Vulture lectured his younger companion. 'I feel the Wotan should have little to fear from air attack.'

'Providing we observe strict blackout control, sir,' von Dodenburg answered. 'But what about their naval bombardment?'

The Vulture frowned. 'I think we'll manage to scrape through underneath it. We can assume that the naval bombard-

* Von Rundstedt's HQ just outside Paris. (Transl.)

ment will hit the rear areas behind the Battery first, trying to cut it off from reinforcements. Then it'll move to the immediate vicinity of the Battery to cover their infantry going in. I think we'll make it before then.'

'I'll buy that, sir. But all the same, I don't like this road.' He indicated the white gleaming causeway, bordered on both sides by high thick hedges.

'What do you mean?' the Vulture looked suspiciously at him as they began to trot into Belleville-sur-Mer.

'Plenty of cover on both sides. No room for manoeuvre for anybody on the road itself, sir. In other words, sir, a perfect place for an ambush.'

'We'll be at the Battery before the Tommies can get this far, von Dodenburg.'

'It wasn't the Tommies I was thinking of, sir. I was thinking of the French.'

'The French!' the Vulture laughed; it wasn't a very pleasant sound. 'My dear Major, the French are an efficiently decadent people and suitably selfish as such people usually are. Unlike the absurd English and Germans who seem to find pleasure in killing each other, the French occupy themselves more realistically with the joys of the flesh. This,' he made an obscene gesture, 'and this,' he slapped his lean stomach with his free hand. 'Why should they risk their precious French necks for a bunch of skinny-ribbed, buck-teethed Tommies? No, no, my dear Major, the French have long forgotten the war and got on with the business of living.'

'All the same, sir,' von Dodenburg began, but stopped suddenly. The Vulture's gaze was directed on the beach which had revealed itself to the right and below them.

Kuno von Dodenburg reined in his horse and stared at the narrow shelving beach covered with heavy shingle. Beyond it rose a sheer white cliff, its only outlet a narrow, steep-sided gully, filled to a depth of two metres with barbed and rabbit wire. The wire was stretched very tight and pinioned to iron stakes driven into the sides of the gully. 'It looks very formidable, sir,' he ventured.

The Vulture nodded slowly. 'Yes, it does. If the Tommies ever got their eggs caught on that, there'd be a few singing tenors about.' He jerked the reins. 'Let's go and have a look at the Battery.'

They trotted on, past a large, lonely white house perched on the edge of the cliff, which looked like an abandoned church.

'Mg nest,' the Vulture observed as they reined their horses once again and took in the Goebbels Battery.

Von Dodenburg knew the details of the Battery by heart now. It had been built by the French in 1936, as part of the coastal defences. After 1940 and the start of the Tommy commando raids, the Wehrmacht had improved it so that its guns had a maximum range of 22,000 metres. Each of its guns was mounted on a thick ferro-concrete platform, revolving on a central pivot, defended against infantry attack by thick wire fences and seven mg posts, each manned by five men under the command of a corporal. To the rear of the guns there were two further mg posts with magnificent fields of fire over a couple of hundred metres of open country flanked by woodland. The whole place was garrisoned by some two hundred artillerymen.

The Vulture licked his thin lips carefully. 'Not bad, not bad at all, von Dodenburg. But mind you the garrison is artillery and you know my feelings about the devotees of Saint Barbara?'*

'No, sir.'

The Vulture grinned. 'All big heads and big arses. All brains and not much pepper in their pants when it comes to action.'

Kuno von Dodenburg smiled. He knew why the Vulture disliked the artillery; their officers, the intellectual cream of the Wehrmacht, got promotion even quicker than the Armed SS, and everything the Vulture did was subordinated to be-

* Patron saint of the artillery.

coming a general as his father had been before him. 'All the same, behind those defences they won't need much pepper in their pants on the day, sir,' he remarked.

'I suppose not,' the Vulture said, stroking his monstrous nose. 'All in all, the place looks good. It'll hold till we arrive here when the Tommies land.'

'*If*, sir,' von Dodenburg persisted.

'You're still worried about that road?'

'Yessir.'

'All right, von Dodenburg what do you suggest I should do about it?'

'Well, sir, I'd feel happier if we had the Battalion's armour standing by to cover us if anything went wrong.'

'It won't,' the Vulture said.

'If they were alerted at the same time as the infantry, they could reach us within minutes of trouble, the Major persisted.

'The crews are only half trained, you know! They'd probably do more damage to each other than to the enemy in the dark.'

'I don't care, sir, I'd feel happier if we had them standing by in case of emergency.'

The Vulture looked hard at the younger officer's handsome, serious face. 'You know, von Dodenburg, you are going to worry yourself into an early grave.'

'Better that than a Tommy bullet, sir,' von Dodenburg said, smiling.

'All right, you win. The armour will be alerted. But God only knows what will happen when those greenbeaks get behind the wheels of the Mark IVs.'

*   *   *

That evening the Laird of Abernockie and Dearth staggered from the DR's motorbike, his face and uniform covered in thick white dust and moved stiffly to the entrance of Combined Ops HQ in Richmond Terrace. Thickly he demanded to be allowed to see Lord Louis Mountbatten.

'But you can't expect to see the Admiral just like that, Colonel,' the elegant aide replied horrified. 'He's a very busy man, you know.'

'Listen, mate,' the Commando Colonel snapped, 'if I'm not in there talking to his Lordship within the next five minutes I'll have them nifty upper class knackers off yer with my winkle-picker,' his hand dropped to the skean dhu tucked into his stocking top, 'in no seconds nothing.'

The elegant aide hurried away.

'It's the Commander of the Seventh Commando, sir,' he explained hurriedly to an amused Mountbatten, 'and he's in a devil of a mood. He threatened to – well, it doesn't matter, sir.'

Mountbatten laughed. 'Old A and D, eh?' he exclaimed. 'The 'orror of the 'ighlands! Oh well, let him come, I can let him have five minutes, Jenkins.'

The diminutive Colonel in the drooping, dusty kilt got down to business at once. 'Admiral, I don't like it – I don't like it one bit!'

'What don't you like, A and D?'

'The whole op – this bloody Operation Jubilee.' He leaned forward across the big desk, his shaggy carrot-red hair falling over his forehead. 'I think the Jerries have rumbled us.'

Mountbatten's handsome face hardened. 'Impossible,' he said firmly in his best quarterdeck manner.

'Well, what about these SS troops doing speed marches on the road between Braquemont to Berneval, Admiral? Why that particular stretch of road in the whole of France, eh?'

'Coincidence, A and D.'

'Get off, Admiral,' the Laird of Abernockie and Dearth snorted irreverently. 'Pull the other leg – it's got bells on it!'

'What do you mean, Colonel?'

'Well, just look at the whole ruddy set-up, Admiral. Jubilee was first scheduled for April 1942. Then there were about

69

fourteen hundred second-grade Jerry soldiers in Dieppe. By July when we had originally planned to launch Jubilee, there were three divisions in the area, including a sodding SS division.' He looked accusingly at Mountbatten, but the Admiral remained stonily silent.

'All right, what happened then?' the Colonel continued. 'The op was cancelled and what did the old Hun do – he withdraws some of the troops.' He raised a dirty finger warningly. 'But that wasn't the end of it, oh no, Admiral. As soon as the op is on again, the Jerries move back. What's going on over there? Has old von Rundstedt got a yo-yo up his arse, or – do the Jerries know we're coming?' The Laird of Abernockie and Dearth breathed out hard and stopped suddenly. With fingers that trembled slightly with surpressed rage, he lit another of his favourite Woodbines.

Mountbatten hesitated. The comic Colonel was not the first to have protested against Operation Jubilee that week. General Montgomery who had been in charge of the operation originally had written from his new command in the Desert to General Paget, C-in-C Home Forces, 'if they want to do something on the Continent, let them chose another target than Dieppe'. It was obvious that a group within the Army was rapidly losing confidence in the whole nasty business; yet Mountbatten knew how desperately Churchill was pushing the op – and his own star was linked to that of the Prime Minister.

'A and D,' he began finally, 'I think you are concerning yourself unduly about all this.' He shrugged. 'Couldn't we call them a series of coincidences that mount up to exactly nothing.'

'You might. I don't!' the little Colonel replied bluntly. 'I'm responsible for the lives of four hundred men, I can't afford to lark around with coincidences. You of all people should understand. They're my people, I'm their Laird.'

Mountbatten would have laughed on any other occasion at the comparison. But at this moment the irate little Colonel presented too much of a danger. He would not feel himself bound by the caste loyalty of the regular officer. He might well just go and blow his fears to some damn reporter on the *Daily Mirror*, and then there would be the very hell to play. 'Yes, I understand, A and D, but what exactly do you expect me to do? The Op begins on Tuesday night. Too many people and too many things are involved. It is too late to make any drastic alterations to the plan now.'

'I don't know about that, Admiral,' the Colonel persisted doggedly. 'I'm only concerned about my lads. Now, let's just assume that them ruddy Jerries marching up to Berneval every other day, as Intelligence states, are the ones who are gonna support the Battery when my chaps move in.'

Mountbatten opened his mouth to protest, but the Laird was quicker. 'Give us a bit o' hush, Admiral and let me finish, will you? Let's assume I'm right. So what happens to my lads when the initial bombardments alerts the Jerries that something is up? I'll tell you,' he pointed his finger at the elegant, square-jawed scion of princes. 'The Jerries'll catch them with their knickers down, hanging on that ruddy big cliff under the Battery. And it won't be penny buns they'll start throwing at us – it'll be handfuls of shit. Now, all I'm asking for me and the lads is that you take care that those SS men don't get to the Battery before we do. We're prepared to take our chance after that, Admiral.'

Mountbatten's brain raced and he reacted as quickly as he had ever done on the pre-war polo field. 'All right, A and D,' he snapped, reaching out for his red-painted scrambler phone, 'I'll take care of your SS men. You worry about that damned Battery. Now then would you excuse me, A and D, I've got a lot to do before Tuesday morning.'

TEN

'Silence in the whorehouse!' Sergeant-Major Metzger bellowed at the top of his tremendous voice.

Silence fell on the assembled NCOs of the First SS Assault Battalion Wotan. Slowly the Butcher ran his piglike little eyes around the NCOs' red, gleaming expectant faces, their big hams already curled round the handles of their beer-mugs in anticipation. Satisfied with their appearance, he raised his glass with ceremonial slowness, until it reached the third button of his tunic as was prescribed in the regulations.

'Comrades of the NCO Corps,' he snapped formally. 'It gives me great pleasure to welcome you to our *Kameradschaftsabend*.* Up the cups, comrades.'

The one hundred and fifty NCOs raised their mugs to the level of their third button, slopping beer everywhere.

'I know it's only French gnat's piss,' the Butcher bellowed. 'But it's gonna be a cold night, *prost*!'

Like automatons, the NCOs guzzled the frothy French beer sucking it down in noisy gulps until their mugs were empty. Then, as the traditional Army ceremony prescribed, they banged the mugs down on the scrubbed wooden tables and rubbed the bases round three times in noisy unison.

The Butcher wiped the foam from his mouth with the back of his hairy hand, his face already beginning to sweat in the August heat. He looked at Schulze. 'Sergeant Schulze,' he barked, a smirk on his broad face, 'you reckon yourself the Battalion comic, tell us a joke.'

'And make it a juicy one, Schulze,' chuckled Sergeant Gross, who made a habit of chewing razor blades when he was

* Roughly equivalent to a British Army 'smoker'.

drunk. 'I always get a stiff one when I hear a juicy one, pox-cop.'

Schulze, his face angry and glowering, stumbled awkwardly to his feet. He thrust up his plastered paw. 'Why don't yer sit on that, Gross,' he snorted. 'Give yerself a cheap thrill! A joke, Sergeant Major? What about the two nuns practising hymns together in bed?'

'Eh?' the Butcher looked at him blankly.

'Shit,' breathed Matz, sitting next to Schulze, 'that bastard's so dumb he can't even eat soup with a spoon.'

'Well, what about the one of the plastic surgeon who hanged himself?' Schulze persisted.

'You call that a shitty joke?' the Butcher growled. 'Give us one to make us laugh. We don't want those lemons, you rooting sow. We want something to make us piss our pants!'

Schulze looked up at the ceiling desperately, as if appealing to God to snatch him away from so many fools. 'Well, Sergeant Major,' he said carefully, trying the joke he had told on these occasions for the last three years, 'did you hear what the soldier said to his missus on his first night home after six months away from her?'

'No,' the Butcher said eagerly; the French waitresses had almost finished refilling the glasses now.

'Take a good look at the floor, darling, *because you're not gonna be seeing anything except the ceiling for the next shit-ting forty-eight hours!*'

The room exploded with laughter, while Schulze stared at his comrades' red sweating faces with undisguised disgust. 'Now that's what I call a joke, Schulze!' the Butcher gasped, tears running down his face. He grasped his mug. 'All right, comrades, let's sink this one before it gets too cold. *Kamera-den – prost!*'

Schulze looked out of the window at the brilliant, sun-drenched square, and hissed through his beer, 'Matzi, don't swallow so much o' that parrot pee. Remember we've got better things in front of us.' He smiled, remembering the revenge he would be soon taking on Sergeant-Major shitty Metzger, and winked at Matz.

The one-legged NCO winked solemnly back.

*   *   *

The same brilliant sunshine that shone down on the barracks of Assault Battalion Wotan that Tuesday afternoon, 18th October 1942 scorched the roads of Southern England·too, transforming the long lines of vehicles queuing up outside the ports into stifling boxes. They rumbled past ancient, stub-towered Saxon churches and squeezed through narrow cobbled high streets towards the gleaming green stretch of water below. Here and there grubby children in ragged shirts, making tar horses from matchsticks and the melted tar at the roadside, waved. But their mothers, emaciated, long deprived of their husbands, their hair in iron curlers, stared at the convoys apathetically. They had seen too many men drive down to the ports never to return during these last black years.

Now the little south coast ports were filled with marching Canadians, their transports left above on the heights overlooking the boats. *Essex Scottish Regiment ... Fusiliers Mont-Royal ... Royal Hamilton Light Infantry ... Queen's Own Cameron Highlanders of Canada ...* Five thousand of them, marching through silent streets scrawled with the fading 'SECOND FRONT NOW!' slogans, echoing to the stamp of steel-shot ammunition boots.

Nobody waved. Nobody shouted. No bands played. And it was fitting that they didn't. For of the five thousand men crunching over the cobbles, swinging their arms fiercely, sweating in the hot afternoon sun, only two thousand would ever see England again.

*   *   *

74

'*Meine Herren*,' said the Vulture, 'I know it is hot, but may I crave your attention?' He looked at the Wotan officers with barely concealed boredom.

The Wotan officers, clad in black breeches and their white summer jackets, faced their red-faced CO.

'In a moment we shall be going across to the NCOs' Mess to endure yet another of those social evenings which the *Reichsheini* with his petty-bourgeois weakness for such impossible occasions, has forced upon us.' The Vulture looked challengingly at his officers to check whether any of his National Socialist fanatics were prepared to take offence at his remarks about their Supreme Leader. But they feared him, more than they respected Himmler and they remained silent.

Von Dodenburg smiled to himself. The Vulture had really tamed the Battalion's Party hotheads. A mere twelve months ago, he himself would have taken offence at remarks of that kind. But that had been before Russia.

'Now I do not know your capacity for strong waters. All I know is that the gentlemen of the SS NCO Corps will undoubtedly drink themselves into insensibility this evening in their usual piggish fashion. My officers will *not* do so, however much they are pressed to do by those guzzling swine over there.' He waved his riding crop in the direction from which the first and inevitable chorus of *Oh, du schoener Westerwald* was coming. 'You will accept a maximum of three schnapps – in the case of you younger lieutenants a sniff at the waitress's apron should suffice – and that is all. The Tommies could land at any moment and I don't want any of you getting your turnips blown off because your brains were too schnapps-addled to react fast enough.' He laughed harshly and fingered his Knight's Cross. 'After all, I need you alive so that I can cure my throatache with a few diamonds.'

A few of the older officers laughed, but not many. The Vulture was deadly serious. He would sacrifice them all if it would gain him the coveted 'diamonds' for his Knight's Cross.*

Kuno von Dodenburg walked out into the brilliant sunshine with his CO and blinked his eyes rapidly. The hot glare cut at his eyeballs like a sharp knife.

'Phew,' he breathed and wiped away the sweat. 'Do you think they'll really come in this heat, sir?'

'They can cool off in the sea when we kick them back into it,' the Vulture said, apparently unaffected by the temperature. He levelled his cane at the flat oily-slow swell of the water below. 'Ideal for a landing, that sea. For all we know, my dear Major they may be beyond the horizon at this very moment.' He laughed and allowed von Dodenburg to open the door to the NCOs' party.

*   *   *

It was now 6.10 p.m. With a soft plop the buoy with its green flag slipped into the calm sea from the leading ship of the Royal Navy's 13th Minesweeping Flotilla. The first marker through the German minefield that barred the way of the invasion fleet to follow had been laid. Swiftly the little minesweepers started to surge forward in a tight V to begin clearing the Channel.

Behind them, in the south coast ports, covered by a thick, choking smoke screen, the troopships, disguised all these weeks as merchant ships, began to shed their camouflage. The soldiers began to march up the gangplanks, labelled and numbered like a package. In the galleys the sweating, dirty cooks in their torn undershirts started to hand out the last supper many of the troops would ever eat.

'Sodding hell,' Colonel the Laird of Abernockie and Dearth cursed, looking down at the greasy mess at the bottom of his mess-tin, 'ruddy soya links and cowboy beans. Trust the Navy to make sure that us brown jobs spill our guts before we ever

* The very rare additional class of the Knight Cross. (Transl.)

76

sodding well get there!'

'Oh, I don't know, sir,' Freddy Rory-Brick answered imperturbably, spooning up his beans, 'it's weally wather good!'

* * *

As the officers led by the Vulture entered and the assembled NCOs stamped to their feet, Schulze whispered to the plump, big-breasted waitress Marie, with whom he had been sleeping the last few nights, 'Come over here, Juicy.'

'Why do you call her Juicy?' Matz queried.

'If you had your dirty big paw where I've got mine just now,' Schulze answered, 'you'd know why.'

'Filthy bugger!' Matz said disgustedly, as Marie giggled with delight.

Schulze had to hurry if he were to carry out his plan successfully this evening. He passed the waitress the phial of liquid he had stolen from the bone-menders that afternoon.

Juicy giggled again when she saw the dark brown bottle. 'The boom-boom?' she queried, eyes sparkling.

'Very boom-boom,' Schulze said mysteriously. 'That stuff should go off like Vesuvius exploding.'

Still giggling, the waitress went off, leaving Matz looking at Schulze in bewilderment. 'What's all this, Schulze?' he asked, when they had taken their seats again, and the officers with them.

Schulze chuckled with undisguised joy. 'It's concentrated brown bomber for the Butcher,' he exclaimed.

Matz's mouth fell open. Like everyone else in the Battalion, he feared the tremendously powerful laxative that had been dreamed up by the fiendish Doctor Hackenschmitt, Wotan's new surgeon. 'Shit, Schulze, one drop of that stuff makes yer fart like a flamethrower!'

'Exactly, my little crippled friend,' Schulze replied calmly, raising his glass in false comeraderie to the Butcher, whose big hand was now gripping the doctored beer.

The Butcher let his attention wander from the Vulture's conversation and took a mighty swig.

Schulze nudged Matz in the ribs. Matz spewed a mouthful of beer on to the table. 'What yer shittingly well doing?' he gasped, 'trying to break me ribs?'

'He's drunk it,' Schulze whispered urgently. 'The Butcher's drunk it! Now we'll have a few fireworks.'

'But what's all this in aid of?' Matz demanded. 'What yer giving him the brown bomber for?'

'Cos we want to get out of here without trouble.'

'Leave a free piss-up!' Matz exploded.

'There are higher things, Corporal Matz,' Schulze said solemnly.

'Tell me one.'

'C-U-N-T,' Schulze spelled out the word slowly.

Matz's sullen look vanished. 'Oh, well, that's something different,' he agreed heartily. 'I didn't realise we were talking about religion. But where?'

'The Café de la Belle Alliance.'

'Rosi-Rosi, Schulze! But she's the Butcher's piece. If we buggered off now and he found you in the pit with her later on, he'd have the eggs off'n yer with a blunt razor-blade.'

'My poor simple soldier,' Schulze said pityingly, 'tonight the Navy's out on an exercise, this lot here are getting pissed and soon Sergeant-Major Metzger will suffer an unfortunate accident which will keep him close to his personal thunderbox for the rest of the night. So, Matzi, what do you conclude from that?'

'That you'll be able to shove yer meat into Rosi-Rosi and I'll have the pick of her whores.' Matz rubbed his hand delightedly. 'I might spoil myself tonight with a couple of 'em.'

'Come on, let's sneak out, Matz.'

Carefully the two of them pushed back their chairs and strolled with apparent casualness towards the door.

'Hello, where are you two going?'

It was Major von Dodenbuug, a glass of beer, hardly touched, in his hand.

'It's Matz, sir,' Schulze rose to the occasion immediately. 'He's got a touch of migraine. I think it's the company,' he added. 'The noise and the rough talk.'

Matz looked wan.

'I think I'll get the little feller back to his bunk, and settle him down with Goethe's poems and a cup of weak tea.'

Von Dodenburg grinned and pulled down the corner of his right eye. 'Can you see any green there, Schulze? Now what are you two –'

He stopped as the head of the table was shattered by a tremendous burst of wind, which set the glasses rattling. The Vulture's monocle popped out of his eye with surprise. It was only with difficulty that he restrained himself from falling backwards. Seated next to him, Sergeant Gross grabbed his throat frantically, eyes crossed dramatically. 'Gas alarm!' he cried as if he were choking. 'Gas alarm!'

As the Butcher staggered to his feet, his face a sickly green, his hands clutched to his ominously rumbling stomach, Schulze said hastily: 'I think we'd better be going now, sir. And I'd advise you not to stay too long, there are a lot of rough types about!'

*   *   *

Von Dodenburg watched them stagger down the road towards Dieppe, their bodies shaking uncontrollably. Then he shrugged and dismissed them from his mind. Slowly he crunched a path across the fine grey gravel of the parade ground towards the First Company area. Already the night was beginning to slide long black fingers across the ground. Soon it would be time for the men in the barracks to put up the blackouts. He dropped the cheap Dutch cigar that someone had offered him at the NCO's party and ground it out, staring at the youthful, unlined, unspoiled faces of his men, their cheeks tan-

79

ned and glowing with good health, their gestures quick and assured. Suddenly he felt a warm glow of pride in them. The drunken cries, roars, snatches of dirty songs coming from the NCO's party were forgotten. There was no dirtiness, no corruption here, von Dodenburg told himself. Here there was only dedicated devotion to Folk, Fatherland and Führer. Here was the new Germany, unburdened by the dirty compromises of the past, the clean young men who would run the Reich when the war was won.

Warmed by the thought, Major Kuno von Dodenburg yawned hugely and then turning, began to make his way back to his own quarters. He was suddenly very tired. He would make an early night of it. Tomorrow would be another day.

*　　*　　*

They were through the minefield. There was a half moon and the sea was as smooth as glass. But the faint rustle of the wind and the lapping of the waves covered the stir of the ships' screws and the subdued yet precise snap of commands. Everything was running smoothly. Yet there was a taut quality of suspense everywhere. For the CO of the 7th Commando it was as though it were his first raid and the first time he had crept through the undergrowth towards an unsuspecting German sentry. He took another sip of ration whisky from his silver flask and offered it to Freddy.

'What do you think?' he asked softly, as if on the invisible enemy coast, German soldiers were straining their ears to catch his words.

'The usual balls-up, sir, I wouldn't be suwpwised.'

'The lads okay?'

'Oh, I wouldn't know, sir,' Freddy answered easily. 'I leave that sort of democwatic stuff of the NCOs.'

'Big streak o' piss,' the Colonel said severely. 'Gimme that flask back, you glutton.'

For a moment the two officers were silent as the fleet of 250 little ships started to form up into groups for the final leg of the voyage to the French coast. Freddy Rory-Brick focused the borrowed night glasses and for want of something better to do began to count them aloud.

'Five ... six ... seven ... ten ... eleven ... twelve ...' Suddenly he stopped.

'What's up, Freddy?' the Colonel asked casually, finishing the last of the Scotch.

Freddy hesitated.

'Well come on, pee or get off the pot!'

'It's the gwoups, sir,' Freddy answered unhappily.

'What about them?'

'Well.' Again he hesitated.

'Oh, come on Freddy, get yer bleeding upper-class finger out, will you! We'll be in sodding France by the time you get it out – the way you're going on.'

'It's the number of groups sir.' He licked salt-dry lips almost fearfully. 'There are thirteen of them.'

ELEVEN

'Shit on the shingle!' Schulze had exclaimed delightly, pressing the rouged nipples of her tremendous breasts in his hairy ears. 'God, I'm going deaf – I can't hear a fucking thing!'

That had been the last thing he had said before he had passed out, exhausted by too much love-making and drunk with the *Marc* she had fed him purposefully all the night.

Now Rosi-Rosi gently released his big snoring face from between her naked breasts. With surprising agility, she slipped out of the double bed and opened the door to the bedroom.

The cafe was silent. It had been a quiet night and most of the whores had left early complaining about the lack of business. Now there was no sound except the big German sergeant snoring, and a soft regular squeak higher up where presumably his one-legged companion was still occupied with Claude and Gi-gi.

'Jo-Jo,' the whore called softly. 'Are you awake?'

Her diminutive lover appeared from behind the zinc-topped bar. 'Is the Boche pig asleep?' he whispered.

She nodded. 'Snoring as if he were sawing down a forest.'

Jo-Jo yawned and helped himself to a pernod from the half-empty bottle on the counter. 'Good, it's about time for the Englishman to come.'

Rosi-Rosi picked up an apron. Jo-Jo grinned sleepily as she bound it round her naked stomach. 'What's the matter – do you think the Englishman has never seen one of those hairy things before?'

'*Salaud!*' she cursed calmly and shrugged, her breasts trembling like puddings as she did so: 'You never know with the

82

English,' she said. 'They are a very virginal people.' She strode over to the bar and poured herself a glass of beer. She sank it in one gulp and belched contentedly. 'Why do you think he wants to see us tonight, Jo-Jo?'

Jo-Jo shrugged his skinny, consumptive's shoulders. 'Who knows? He is a man who keeps to himself. They all are.' He sipped his pernod pensively. 'You know, Rosi-Rosi,' he said, 'if I had to choose between the English and the Boche, I'd pick the latter.'

'Why?'

'They spend more money. The milords were very tight with their money here in Dieppe before the war.' He looked at her massive naked bulk seriously. 'The Germans are a very generous people, on the other hand.'

Rosi-Rosi put her hand to the base of her stomach. 'Well, if they are all like that big bull upstairs, they're generous all right – not only with their money!'

Jo-Jo opened his mouth to reply, but the woman stopped him with a quick gesture of her plump, beringed hand. 'The bike,' she hissed. 'It's him!'

They listened tensely to the faint metallic sound of a bicycle being propped up outside, followed a second later by a single tap on the door – the signal. 'Open up, Jo-Jo, quick!' Rosi-Rosi commanded and flicked off the light behind the bar.

Rosi-Rosi waited till the man had entered and the door was closed again, before she turned on the light once more.

'I say!' the Englishman exclaimed, his blue eyes dropping on to her naked, berouged breasts.

'*Comment?*' Rosi-Rosi asked, not understanding his English. The SOE* man, a tall, slim captain with quick nervous eyes and a permanent tic in his right cheek, said in his rapid, excellent French. 'Nothing. It just slipped out, Madame.'

'That's what that Boche pig upstairs kept saying last night,'

* Special Operations Executive, a branch of British Intelligence. (Transl.)

83

Rosi-Rosi said sourly.

'What?' the SOE Captain looked at her puzzled.

'Nothing. But what do you want to see us for at this time of night?'

For a moment the Englishman overcame his acute nervousness, the result of six months of undercover living, running the Dieppe network, and smiled. 'They're coming,' he announced proudly.

'Who's coming?' Jo-Jo asked.

'We are – the British! We are attempting a great landing this morning. Out at the points, and here. You will see,' he added. 'It will be something to tell your grandchildren about.'

Rosi-Rosi made an obscene gesture with her upraised middle finger, which gave eloquent testimony to what she thought of history, and cried. '*Here!* Did you say *here*?'

'Shh!' hissed the SOE officer. 'Yes, when we have taken both batteries we shall land in force on Dieppe Plage. Once they have overcome the Promenade defences, they'll be coming straight up the *Marechal Foch* and *Verdun*. You'll find yourself right in the middle of a battle, if you stay, Madame.'

'If I *stay, sale con*,' Rosi-Rosi cried furiously. 'Where do you think I'm going? I'm not going to sacrifice my property, my beautiful cafe, for any damned war.' Tears of self-pity and anger welled up in her blood-shot eyes. 'Why didn't you tell us this when you involved us in your silly damn spy game?'

The SOE Captain looked at her incredulously. 'But it's for your country, Madame,' he protested. 'We are coming to liberate you from the German yoke.'

'Stick your liberation up your skinny English arse!' she sobbed through her tears.

'But you must go now. I came here specially to warn you. I have other more important tasks to carry out before this night is finished,' the SOE officer said fervently and tried to lay his hand on Rosi-Rosi's naked shoulder.

She shook it off angrily. 'Get your paws off me!' she

84

screamed. 'Who told you to touch me? You've ruined me, you have, and I've got the best knocking shop in Dieppe.'

'*Ssh!*' Jo-Jo hissed urgently. 'You'll wake the Boche!'

But it was too late. The Boche was already awake, standing stark naked at the top of the stairs, his usually happy face set in stony disbelief. Schulze had not been able to understand very much of the French but what he had been able to understand had sufficed. He knew he was in the presence of the Resistance.

He towered above them, a great bull of a man, the reason he had awoke and sought her wilting away rapidly before their startled eyes. Sergeant Schulze had never had any dealings with spies before, and he was at a loss. But he knew he should do something.

The British officer made up his mind for him by moving his hand to the shoulder of his shabby jacket. Schulze was a shade quicker. With a great roar, he launched himself into the air. The SOE officer screamed as Schulze's flying bulk descended upon him. The SOE officer went suddenly stiff as his face twisted at an awkward angle. His neck was broken.

Jo-Jo rushed at Schulze with a knife clasped tightly to his side. Schulze skipped behind a table. Jo-Jo lunged. Schulze brought down his white club of a right hand. Jo-Jo screamed with pain, as Schulze pinned him to the table. 'Let go ... let go, you're breaking my wrist!'

The cry alarmed a hitherto mesmerized Rosi-Rosi. With a wild cry she sprang on to Schulze's back, and wrapping her plump arms around his neck, dug her heels into his naked ribs as if she were riding a horse.

'Get off,' Schulze yelled thickly, as Jo-Jo freed his hand and lunged again.

He felt the knife slice his ribs. Desperately he spun round, trying to shake Rosi-Rosi's great bulk off. But she clung to him like an angry limpet. Jo-Jo sucked in a deep breath, his eyes wild. Schulze could see he was coming in for the kill. Fran-

tically he tried to lever Rosi-Rosi's interlocked fingers apart
with his clumsy plastered paws.

'Having a bit of a lark?' Matz's cool voice inquired from
above them.

Schulze flung a wild glance at the head of the stairs. Matz
was poised there, his arms wrapped around the nubile bodies
of the naked girls at either side of him. He was smiling
encouragingly.

'Move, pigshit!' Shulze gasped fervently. 'They're trying to
kill me!'

'Naughty, naughty,' Matz said and bent down, as if he had
all the time in the world.

He gave the girls a quick push to both sides. Unstrapping
his wooden leg in one swift movement, he hurled it once round
his head like a lasso and let go. It hissed through the air. With
a solid, fleshly thwack, it caught Jo-Jo in the face. He went
flying back over the bar, blood squirting in a thick red stream
from his smashed nose, to slam against the wall.

Hopping down the stairs like a naked kangaroo, Matz
grabbed at Rosi-Rosi. She freed one heel and aimed a wild
blow at her new assailant but missed. 'Naughty, naughty,'
Matz commented again.

She screamed shrilly and slackened her grasp on Schulze's
neck. He didn't hesitate. Swinging her round like a sack of
potatoes, he heaved suddenly. Rosi-Rosi lost her grip. With a
wild cry for help, she dropped to the floor and went slithering
across the room to smash against the wall next to her un-
conscious lover.

'Now what do you call this for a piggery, Schulze?' Matz
asked, supporting himself on the table. 'Can't leave you alone
for a minute and you're off starting orgies or something!' He
grinned.

'Button it!' Schulze snapped, in no mood for humour now.
'These Frogs are some sort of spies or something.'

Matz's grin vanished. 'What do you mean?'

Schulze turned to face a groggy Rosi-Rosi, her hair in complete disorder, her massive breasts dangling loosely to her belly. 'Come on, you Frog sow, out with it! What's all this about?'

'Stick yer tongue up yer ass and give yourself a thrill,' she cried.

Schulze hauled back his big fist. 'Forgive me missus,' he cried through gritted teeth. 'But you asked for it.' He smashed his fist directly into her face.

She gave a high scream of agony, spitting out her front teeth. At the top of the stairs the two whores, ashen-faced with shock, screamed in unison.

Schulze concentrated his angry gaze on the bleeding Rosi-Rosi. 'I'm not asking you again – out with it! What's your game here?'

Rosi-Rosi opened her bloody mouth and spat out another tooth.

'*Salaud, putain*,' she began to curse him. But as she did so they heard a powerful explosion out to sea which set the glasses quivering violently in their shelves behind the bar and rocked the floor beneath the two SS men's naked feet.

'In three devils' name, what was that,' yelled Matz, steadying himself on the shaking table.

'I'll tell you,' Schulze cried, as a blood-red light flooded in through the un-blacked out windows above. 'It's the shitting Tommies. They're here!'

'The Wotan!' Matz gasped. 'They'll need us!'

'You're telling me. Those wet-tails of the First Company are dead ducks without us.'

'But what can we do – me with my leg and you with your flippers, Schulze?'

The women were forgotten, as Schulze cast around desperately for a way out. 'Here,' he cried, 'pick up that peg-leg of yours.' Hurriedly he laid his plastered paws across the table, while Matz hopped to his leg and seized it firmly with both hands. 'Right. Give them a right old bang!'

Matz needed no urging. As the firing grew louder, he brought the booted heel of the wooden leg down across Schulze's outstretched hands.

'By the great whore of Buxtehude, Matzi!' Schulze roared in pain. 'You rotten little perverted banana-sucker, you, what are you trying to do – shear my shitty flippers off!'

But his anger vanished when he saw the long cracks running down each dirty plaster cast. Hastily he slapped the casts together. The paster fell away easily to reveal two pale, terribly wrinkled hands.

'*Ugh!*' Matz exclaimed. 'Those flippers of yours look as if you've just dug 'em up from the boneyard!' Schulze groped for his pistol with fingers which felt like thick cold sausages.

'What you do?' Rosi-Rosi cried in alarm, her eyes wide with fear, her pudgy hands held in front of her great dugs.

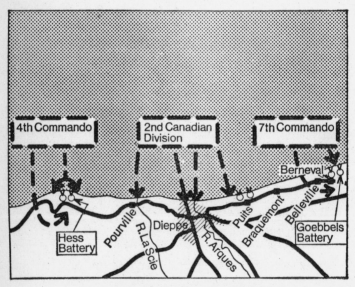

The Attack, August 18/19th, 1942

With a curse Schulze dropped the pistol on the table. 'I was always soft-hearted,' he said, beginning to struggle hurriedly into his clothes. 'Come on, you little shit,' he ordered Matz, as the boom of artillery out to sea grew louder, 'strap on that peg-leg of yourn at the double. Wotan's off to the shitty wars again.'

BOOK TWO: THE BATTERY

'War's hell, but peacetime will shitting well kill you!'
Sergeant Schulze to Corporal Matz, 18th August 1942.

ONE

It was nearly dawn. Out at sea angry red lights blinked on the horizon like enormous blast furnaces. Continuous scarlet flashes split the grey haze. The air shook with the silent detonations of shells. Somewhere out in the Channel the naval battle which had alerted the Wotan was gathering ferocity.

But the gasping, sweat-lathered young SS troopers had no eyes for the sea. Their wide, staring gaze was fired straight ahead: on the crazily heaving shoulders of the man in the next rank in front. For the Vulture was setting a cracking pace. They were now within a kilometre of the Goebbels Battery and the bandy-legged little CO knew it was imperative that Wotan reached the guns before the Tommy barrage descended upon the coastal roads.

'*Tempo-tempo!*' he cried hoarse, as he doubled back down their ranks, slashing at laggards with his riding crop, booting the heavier-set, ashen-faced NCO's, still sick from the night's carousing. 'In three devils' name, will you men never move!'

'We're on time sir,' von Dodenburg gasped, as the Vulture joined him at the head of the column. 'We're making it.'

'Of course, we'll make it,' the Vulture snapped. 'If I have to beat every single one of them into a run. March or croak is Wotan's motto.'

Now the dark low silhouette of Belleville began to loom up ahead. Von Dodenburg recalled his former fears about the village and tightened his grip on his machine-pistol slung across his chest. But the village seemed dead, still sunk in its blacked-out, pre-dawn sleep.

'Don't be so damn nervous, von Dodenburg,' said the Vulture irritably. 'There will be no trouble. As I told you –'

He stopped suddenly, for he had heard the unmistakable chug-chug of a French *gazogene** approaching from the direction of the village.

The Vulture acted at once. '*At the double*, von Dodenburg!' he cried. 'You two sergeants follow with the mg! Come on, get the lead out of your breeches!'

The four men swiftly doubled forward ahead of the column. Now the twin blue crosses of the car's blacked-out lights were visible as it came to meet them. The driver must have spotted them too, for he put his foot down on the accelerator.

The Vulture did not hesitate an instant. 'Stop him!' he yelled and pointed his riding crop, his sole weapon, at the twin crosses.

The leading NCO dropped to his knees, his shoulders tensed. The other giant carrying the heavy load of the MG 42 flung it across the NCO's shoulders. The next moment his comrade pressed the trigger and white tracer hissed low straight down the road. The first burst missed, sailing past the car like white golf balls.

'Hit him you horned-ox,' the Vulture cried in exasperation. He brought his cane down across the giant's back. 'Or by God, I'll have the eggs off you with a blunt razor-blade!'

The giant took more careful aim. He squeezed the trigger. The machine-gun chattered at his shoulder. Hot cartridge cases tumbled noisily to the cobbles. The *gazogene* skidded to a sudden stop, effectively blocking the road.

'Come on, von Dodenburg,' the Vulture ordered. 'Let's get the bastard out of the way.'

'*Nicht schiessen! ... nicht schiessen!*' a voice called from the opaque darkness in near perfect German. 'I'm a friend ... friend!'

The two SS officers stopped in mid-stride, as the hatless figure staggered towards them from the car, blood trickling down the side of his head. The Vulture switched on the little

* A wood-burning car. (Transl.)

torch attached to his jacket. In its blue beam they caught a glimpse of a grey uniform.'

'A *Milice*,* sir,' gasped von Dodenburg.

'Yes, *Milice*,' faltered the wounded man as he came level with them. 'Lieutenant Gautier, sir.'

Von Dodenburg caught a glimpse of a dark, almost Jewish face and wrinkled his nose in disgust at the stink of stale garlic; then he snapped: 'What is it, man, why are you holding us up like this?'

'An ambush ... an ambush. They're waiting for you on the Rue Principale.'

Von Dodenburg looked significantly at the Vulture.

The little Colonel ignored him. 'Who is waiting for us – the Tommies?'

'No, sir,' the French officer replied, springing to attention as he recognised the Colonel's stars. 'My people, sir. Those traitors of the *Maquis*. They moved into the village an hour ago, they overwhelmed my people in their sleep. It was just good fortune that I –'

The Vulture waved him to silence with his cane. Behind him the Wotan had halted, the men tensed and nervous in the dark shadows on both sides of the road, yet grateful for a break in that murderous pace. 'We have no time for manoeuvre, Gautier. We must pass through Belleville and we've got only minutes in which to do it.'

Gautier's dark face lit up. 'There is no need for manoeuvre. What do those Maquis gangsters know of tactics? They have barricaded themselves in the houses on both sides of the main road – perhaps some two hundred of them. But their rear is wide open. There are none of them in the parallel road.'

The Vulture's cold-blue eyes lit up. 'Good, then this is what we will do. Captain Holzmann will take in Number Four Company and flank the village on the left. I will attempt a feint along the main road to draw their fire. You, Major von

* Pro-German French para-military formation. (Transl.)

95

Dodenburg will take One and Two Companies and push up that parallel road. When we are all in position, you will attack their rear and roll them up. I shall then pass through the village at the double and on to the Battery. Is that clear?'

'Clear, sir!' von Dodenburg snapped.

'Clear, Colonel,' echoed the swarthy-looking *Milice* officer. To von Dodenburg, it seemed as if the Frenchman were enjoying the situation.

*   *   *

'This way, Major,' whispered the *Milice* officer.

There was something about the fellow's voice which grated on von Dodenburg, but he knew he had no alternative but to follow. With his two companies spread out in a hasty battle formation, he followed their guide into the narrow back street, bordered upon both sides by ancient tightly shuttered houses which stank of age and manure. To von Dodenburg in the lead, it seemed that the steel-shod boots of his men made a devil of a racket. He prayed that the *Maquis* had concentrated their efforts on the main road. Then if Wotan were caught out here in the open, it would be sheer slaughter.

The French Lieutenant seemed to read his thoughts. As the first sections entered the deep shadows, he whispered: 'It would be better perhaps, if I went ahead, just in case.'

'But –' von Dodenburg began. But the Frenchman did not hear. He was already stealing down the alley silently on his thick crêpe soles. Angrily the SS officer slapped the safety catch of his machine-pistol. Nathan Rosenblat, SOE Captain and formerly of Dachau Concentration Camp, his job done, disappeared into the darkness. Von Dodenburg hesitated. What was he to do? He shivered suddenly, although it was warm. Just then the first shutters were flung open at the end of the street, an angry, gruff voice yelled '*en avant ... mort aux boches!*' and he knew they had walked into a trap. The thick wedge of a double-barrelled shotgun was thrust out of the window and roared into blue-red life. The lead man of the first section screamed hideously, as he took the full blast in his face.

'Stand fast!' von Dodenburg cried desperately, as the shutters were thrust open on both sides of the street and murderous fire erupted from each window. Everything was blood-soaked chaos. Men dropped to the cobbles. '*Stretcher-bearer ... stretcher-bearer ... they've got me in the guts ... Comrades, I'm blinded ... someone help me ... I'M BLINDED!*' The hysterical cries rose on all sides, as the shouting, sweating men in the windows poured a relentless fire into the SS troopers trapped below.

A great plough horse broke out of a stable. Foam bubbled from its slack lips as it clattered through the carnage, its eyes wild with terror. It struck von Dodenburg standing there in the middle of the bloody alley a glancing blow. He reeled back and fired from the hip. The wild burst caught a grenade-thrower in the chest and nearly sawed him in half. He plummeted from the window and hit the bloody cobbles with a soft thud.

Aghast at the slaughter of his young volunteers from the Hitler Youth, von Dodenburg acted the only way he knew. '*Sections one, two and three break into the houses on the left!*' he roared above the vicious snap and crackle of small arms fire. '*Sections four, five and six – the houses on the right. At the double!*'

Frantically the troopers began to batter down the doors with their rifle butts and boots, while their comrades tried to cover them, taking murderous casualties all the time. The first door yielded and a group of panic-stricken youngsters tumbled inside. The survivors of the massacre fought each other for cover, clawing their way in out of that terrible fire over the bodies of their dead and dying comrades. The blinded soldier stumbled down the corpse-littered alley, hands outstretched as he felt his way, sobbing bitterly in blood-red tears from the scarlet pits which had once been his eyes. Von Dodenburg knew he could not leave him. As section after section broke into the houses and began to return the enemy fire, von Dodenburg darted forward, crouched low, firing crazily to both sides. The *Maquis* concentrated its fire on him. Lead stitched blue sparks on the cobbles on both sides. But he seemed to bear a charmed life. '*Over here!*' he gasped wildly.

'Where, sir?' the boy called recognising his voice.

'*To me!*'

Head raised high and at an angle, the boy stumbled through the welter of bodies towards his CO. A Frenchman at one of the windows raised his arm and casually lobbed out a grenade. It landed just in front of the blinded boy.

'*Achtung!*' yelled von Dodenburg.

The boy did not seem to hear. He staggered right into the explosion and it tore him apart. Like a terrible football, his helmeted head rolled towards von Dodenburg, picking its way neatly through the corpses sprawled everywhere, stopping at the Major's feet.

As a horrified von Dodenburg reeled back to the cover of the nearest house and was seized by eager hands, that terrible sightless stare seemed to follow him accusingly, condemning him for leading these young innocents into the murderous trap of Belleville.

TWO

All was still silent as the Eurekas of Number 7 Commando formed up behind the lean rakish shape of the steam gunboat which would lead them into their attack on the Goebbels Battery. To the Laird of Abernockie and Dearth, who three days before had forced Lord Louis into having Wotan ambushed and who was now quietly vomiting into his vomit bag in the lead Eureka, it seemed that everything was running to schedule. Up front the gunboat was now steaming forward at a steady nine knots, followed by the white V of the Eurekas, while somewhere out in the opaque darkness of the flanks, two further destroyers were supposedly zig-zagging back and forth to add their firepower if trouble came.

But to a green-faced, hollow-eyed Laird, it was clear that their services wouldn't be needed; despite his earlier fears it was obvious that Jerry was not expecting them. Apart from his usual sea-sickness and a soaked kilt, the crossing had gone absolutely without incident. Now the prospect of getting ashore, whatever might be waiting for them there, was becoming definitely more appealing than the heaving seas.

'I say, sir, there she is – Fwance!' Freddy Rory-Brick raised a languid hand and pointed to the dark smudge of the coast which lay ahead.

The Laird tossed his vomit bag over the HQ Eureka's wooden side, splattering some of its contents on the unfortunate signals sergeant crouched beside him. He looked at the black wall of France, stark, silent and menacing, and felt that quickening of the blood he always experienced when he was about to go into action.

'Must you always be so ruddy la-di-da, Freddy,' he snorted,

99

trying to repress his own emotions. 'Here we are landing in enemy territory and all you can say is – "*I say, there she is Fwance.*" Ain't you got no feelings?'

'Never weally thought about it much, sir.'

'I don't know, Freddy,' the Laird sighed and tried to wring some of the seawater out of his bedraggled kilt, 'what have I done to deserve a big toff twit like you?'

Freddy grinned lazily. ' 'Spect I have some good points, sir.'

The minutes passed leadenly. Beside them in the Eureka the eighteen commandos started to give their weapons a last check. The sergeant signaller poised over his set. At the blunt bow, the smooth-faced, eighteen-year-old sub-lieutenant skipper prepared to release the gate which would start them on their mad dash up the cliff once the Eureka had hit the beach. The Laird gave his men a quick survey and was pleased with what he saw: his gillies and petty gangsters from the Gorbals looked tough and ready. They wouldn't let him down.

'What time is it, Freddy?'

'Nearly four, sir.'

'Good, thirty minutes to go.'

Now there was no sound save the steady throb-throb of the Eureka's motors and the slap of the green water on their blunt prow. Thoughtfully, the little Commando leader began to strop his skean dhu on the palm of one hand. But he could not quite conceal the nervous tic in his right cheek. Freddy Rory-Brick noted it and told himself the CO was working himself up to his usual beserk battle-rage; some poor Hun was going to suffer this dawn.

It was zero four-fifteen. They could see the dark mass of the coast quite clearly. Here and there a commando nudged his pal and indicated the stark outline of the lone house on the cliff-top which they recognised from their training. Everything was silent. France was still asleep.

The Laird thrust his dagger into the top of his stocking

again and picked up his rifle. 'All right, me lucky lads,' he exclaimed cheerfully. 'The trip round the pier's over. Stand by!' He looked at the pale-faced sub. 'Snotty, when yon gunboat breaks to the right, I want –'

The star shell exploded directly in front of the little convoy with frightening suddenness. A silver spurt of light and then it climbed high into the sky to hang there, bathing everything below in its icy colour.

'Jerries!' the sergeant signaller gasped. 'Over there to the left!'

The two officers swung round and saw the German E-boats were coming in for the attack at forty knots, their multiple cannon chattering frantically. Ahead the gunboat opened fire. The E-boats increased speed.

'Torpedo!' the Laird cried.

'And another!' Freddy added as another wild flurry of bubbles rose from the water.

Desperately the gunboat tried to avoid the deadly fish, but the first one struck it amidships. It reeled as if punched by a gigantic fist. Scarlet flame leapt a hundred feet in the air. The gunboat came to a halt, ominously listing to one side. But still her guns continued to fire.

As if in command to a secret signal, the E-boats roared round in a huge white arc, cannon chattering again. 20mm shells hissed flatly over the surface of the water, dragging a burning fiery-red tail behind them.

The first Eureka reeled under the cannonfire. Splinters of wood sliced the air and thick white smoke gushed from its shattered engine. Tiny blue flames licked greedily at the wooden stern, as the craft trembled to a halt in the churning sea.

The E-boats circled the stricken Eureka like a pack of timber wolves.

'Oh, my poor lads!' the Laird groaned. 'Where are them bloody destroyers? It's slaughter!'

101

'Yes,' Freddy agreed as calm as ever. 'I fear they've really got us by the short and curlies!' He picked up his rifle and began to fire coolly at the nearest E-boat.

'Bugger that for a lark!' the Laird roared, suddenly in command of himself again. 'Hey, you snotty,' he yelled at the ashen-faced sub-lieutenant. 'Don't stand there like a spare prick at a wedding. Get on to that steering. Zig-zag for the coast!' He spun round. 'Signaller. Hand signal if you can by this light.'

'Sir, I'll try,' answered the sergeant, springing to his feet as the first tracer started to wing its way towards them.

'Signal-scatter and make smoke! It's every man for himself now!'

Bracing himself against the wildly swaying deck the sergeant tried to signal. But it was already too late. The E-boats were well within their formation, churning up and down their ranks in great bursts of water, shooting up craft after craft.

The sergeant screamed and reeled backwards, clutching his face. A burning shell fragment had struck him squarely in the nose and ripped a hole in it.

The Laird lowered him gently. 'Don't worry, Jock, it'll be all right.' But the man was already dead.

'Freddy!' yelled the Laird above the chatter of the enemy cannon and the ear-splitting howl of the E-boats, 'for Chrissake, make smoke – we haven't got a chance otherwise!'

Freddy moved with surprising speed. He sprang to the launcher attached to the bow. Tracer hissed through the air all around him, but he managed to grab the trigger of the first launcher and pull hard. A long cannister sailed into the air.

The smoke cannisters tumbled into the sea, stark black against the ruddy glare of the blazing Eurekas. The young skipper desperately twisted and turned the wheel and headed for the cover. Two more Eurekas followed him. Angrily one of the German E-boats roared after them to finish them off, cannon chattering furiously. But just short of the sudden bank of smoke, it swung round and slowed down, rearing up in the water like a spirited horse.

The Laird breathed out a sigh of relief. 'The bugger daren't come in here in case he collides with one of us,' he cried to his men. 'I think we've –'

'Look out, sir!' a soldier cried. 'Torpedo firing!'

The Laird swung round to see the E-boat lurching as the two-ton fish shot from its sharp bows. The sub-lieutenant swung the Eureka round wildly just in time. The deadly weapon hissed past them, trailing a series of popping bubbles behind it.

'Hurrah!' a cry of heart-felt relief rose spontaneously from the commandos' throats as it flashed by. But froze the next instant on their lips as the torpedo struck the Eureka ahead of them. The HQ commandos ducked as the hot blast slapped their own craft from side to side as if it were a paper boat on a pond. The roar seemed to go for ever. The Laird, crouched like the rest, felt his ears must burst soon. He struggled to breathe, his nostrils full of the acrid smell.

And then it was over. The Laird thrust his head cautiously over the side. The other Eureka had vanished and there was nothing there to reveal that it had ever existed save the booted foot bobbing up and down on the circle of water that marked its passing.

As the smoke enclosed them and the roar and snarl of the E-boats' engines grew fainter, the Laird of Abernockie and Dearth realised his was the only craft left. He had exactly eighteen men, including himself, to tackle the Goebbels Battery.

Sick at heart, hardly recognising his own voice, he said softly, 'All right, snotty, move in. We're going to attack!'

THREE

'What is it, *Tschapperl*?' Adolf Hitler mumbled sleepily, using the contemptuous Bavarian name that he always called his mistress when he was angry with her.

Eva Braun pushed back the lock of dark blonde hair which had fallen over her plump face and said, 'Adolf, they want you – on the telephone. It's urgent. Linge* was just at the door.'

Hitler blinked in the sudden light and sat up with a groan, his dyed black hair tousled from sleep. He had forced his entourage at the 'Mountain', his Bavarian retreat, to sit up with him until two in the morning watching the latest revue film and he was tired.

'But he knows he has orders not to disturb me before ten,' he said grumpily. 'He knows I must have some rest when I'm away from the front. How am I to carry on otherwise, eh?'

'Yes, yes, my poor little cheetah,' Eva Braun humoured him and rubbed her generous naked breasts against his sullen face. 'But it's France. Something to do with a place called Dieppe ... You know me, Adolf, I never understand half these things?' She smiled winningly.

Hitler's sleepiness disappeared. 'What did you say? What was it, woman?'

Eva Braun put her hands in front of her breasts and pouted. 'Dieppe, Linge said, but you don't need to shout at me in that manner –'

'Out of my way!' Hitler thrust her to one side and swung swiftly out of bed. Clad in his absurdly old-fashioned night-shirt (which, despite Eva's protests, he insisted on wearing) he strode over to the scrambler phone, picked it up and barked,

* Hitler's personal valet.

'The Leader.'

'Immediately!' gasped the unknown operator.

There was a slight click and an instant later a well-remembered and heartily disliked voice said, 'Heil Hitler!'

'What is it, Rundstedt?'

'As we estimated, *mein Führer*, the English are landing at Dieppe. They started coming in at four this morning.'

'Details?' Hitler rapped, while behind him Eva Braun yawned luxuriously and picked delicately at one of the chocolates she always kept at his bedside.

'Two main convoys as far as we can gather, with assault troops already being landed in the Varengville–Quiberville area, west of Dieppe.'

'The Hess Battery?'

'Correct, *mein Führer*.'

'And are they making progress?'

'Yes, the Battery is under orders not to maintain stiff resistance. And of course I shall not send reinforcements. Before the killing starts, we must allow the English their little victory.'

Hitler frowned. 'You must not say such things, Rundstedt. The English are a great people. It grieves me greatly to have to kill them. If only that drunken plutocratic Jewish capitalist Churchill would learn sense, we could be allies against the Bolsheviks!'

'I understand, *mein Führer*,' von Rundstedt answered respectfully. He knew that the 'Bohemian Corporal', as he called Hitler contemptuously behind his back, admired his ability as a commander; but he knew too that Hitler would not hesitate to break him as he had broken so many other generals during these last few years. Runstedt could not afford to make a serious mistake.

'And the Goebbels?'

'The details are still vague, *mein Führer*. The E-boats which were sent to intercept the English have not yet radioed back full reports. But from what we do know, my Intelligence here at St Germain concludes that we have destroyed most of the troop transports off Berneval.'

'*Grandios!*' Hitler exclaimed and Eva Braun watched amused as her lover stamped his right foot on the floor. The gesture which looked so impressive when he was booted and in uniform looked absurd in a nightshirt and bare feet. 'But I put it to you, Rundstedt, you must not let the Goebbels Battery fall. It is decisive for our plan.'

'It will not fall,' the Field Marshal answered with the authority of fifty years of command in his voice. 'Tonight I shall take the liberty of calling you again and then, *mein Führer*, I shall report to you that no Englishman remains on the soil of France – *alive*. I promise that.'

'So be it then, my dear Field Marshal. Let the English die in their thousands on the beaches of France at the behest of the Bolshevik beast. It will be a great victory for you and the Reich.'

Hitler put down the phone and stared thoughtfully at his own image in the big mirror opposite the bed.

'Sweet one!' Eva cooed, swallowing her chocolate, and holding out her plump arms towards him, 'come back to bed. I shall get you back to sleep again – soon.' She thrust out the smooth bronzed curve of her stomach and opened her legs provocatively.

Hitler was oblivious to her charms. Already he had stripped himself of his nightshirt to reveal his misshapen genitals and his head was buzzing with new plans. Churchill had been in Moscow only twelve days before for nearly a week. Once the attack had been wiped out, Hitler would ensure that Goebbels told the world Dieppe was a desperate attempt to open a Second Front in Europe, an attempt forced by Stalin on Churchill at the Moscow meeting.

He frowned and wondered if he could make more of it than a propaganda victory. He knew that the drunkard Churchill was just as much of a dictator as he was. But the English Prime Minister still had to contend with Parliament, many of whose members hated him. Was there no way that he could turn the failure at Dieppe into an attack which would enable Churchill's enemies in Westminster to get rid of him?

He pulled on his brown shirt and began tucking it into his breeches. On the bed, Eva Braun sprawled on the silken covers in naked abandon, wide awake now, and bored, munching chocolate after chocolate. Before her she saw stretching another long purposeless day with only the servants to talk to, being hastily hushed out of the way when important people arrived at the *Berghof* lest the outside world learned that the lonely olympian figure of their Leader kept a mistress.

Hitler hesitated in his dressing as a horrifying thought flashed through his mind. What if the British did somehow capture the Goebbels Battery? He shivered, tugged at his breeches and walked slowly over to the picture window. Behind the Alps the sun was already beginning to rise, a blood-red ball flushing the harsh sky pink, while the snow-capped mountains were etched in stark silhouette against the sky. Hitler stared out at the coldly beautiful scene which he loved for its cruel Germanic grandeur.

Speaking to the mountains he asked: 'What if my Wotan does not reach the Battery in time?'

But the only answer from the mountains was the faint hush of the cold wind.

FOUR

'I'm dying,' the Butcher moaned. 'Shitting well croaking before yer eyes!' He looked up at them from his perch on the well-scrubbed wooden seat of his personal thunderbox in the NCOs' latrine and groaned again, his big face green and greasy with sweat.

Outside the Tommy naval guns, making the preliminary offshore bombardment, thundered and the Butcher was mortally afraid, as he always was at the prospect of violent action. Yet he dared not move from his perch.

'Why bother me now, Schulze? Can't you see how bad I am? Great balls of fire, my arse is going to burst at any minute.'

Schulze and Matz looked down unsympathetically at the pain-racked Sergeant-Major. '*See*,' Schulze exclaimed. 'You don't have to see – I can smell it. The green smoke in here is strong enough to make old Matzi's hair curl – if the little cripple had any.'

'Spare me the humour, Schulze,' the Butcher said weakly, wiping the beads of sweat from his forehead with the back of his big hand. 'A big Hamburg dummy like you simply can't understand what pain I'm in.'

Schulze bit back an angry retort. 'Listen Metzger,' he snapped. 'Something's happened to the Battalion at Belleville. There's a lot of shit flying about up there and from here you can see a couple of the Frog houses are burning. I think Wotan is catching a packet.'

'And what am I supposed to do about it?'

'Release those Mark IVs of yours outside.'

'Yeah, send them up that road at the double,' Matz added.

'A couple of 75mms* would sort out the mess.'

The Butcher thrust out both hands, clutching wads of toilet paper, as if he wished to sweep them out of the NCOs' latrine for good. 'Heaven, arse and twine, man,' he cried, 'can't you see I'm about to snuff it? My guts feel as if they're chucking hand grenades about in there.'

'Couldn't happen to a nicer feller,' Matz commented in an aside to his running mate. 'I hope the bastard blows all his gaskets.'

Metzger didn't hear. 'Listen, I can't release those Mark IVs for two reasons. One – the CO says those tanks don't move without his express, personal permission. Two, that bunch of wet-tailed greenbeaks outside, who are supposed to man them, would be about as much use as a peterman in a home for warm brothers. They'd kill each other quicker than they would the Tommies!'

'But Sergeant Major,' Matz protested hotly. 'Perhaps the Vulture ain't in a position to call for the tanks. For all we know he might be up to his big beak in shit at Belleville.'

The Butcher farted, his stomach rolling crazily like the opening to the third act of the *Gotterdammerung*. 'Leave me, I feel another attack coming on.' He gripped the sides of the thunderbox, as if he might be blown off it at any moment, the veins standing out crimson at the temples. Under his sweat-soaked shirt, Schulze could see the muscles of his stomach making alarming involuntary contractions.

'Holy strawsack,' Matz breathed in awe. 'I do believe you're going to give birth in a minute, Sergeant-Major!'

'If I could only find the Frog who brewed that beer we drunk last night,' Sergeant-Major Metzger groaned, the sweat streaming down his broad face in rivulets, 'I'll cut his nuts off with one of his own beer bottles.'

'Metzger,' Schulze cut in. 'Son of whore, what a chance this will be for you! All right, so those wet-tails outside have still

* The calibre of the gun carried by the Mark IV tank. (Transl.)

109

got eggshells behind their spoons. There are three of us, all experienced tankmen. We could run the show on that basis.' He leaned forward eagerly, his blue eyes glowing. 'Imagine it, Metzger, you'll go down in the Wotan's regimental history. Sergeant-Major Metzger, while suffering grievously from the shits, threw himself fearlessly into the battle of Dieppe. When his leg was blown off –'

'He seized it like a club,' Matz continued, 'and waded bravely into the mass of buck-teethed Tommies.'

'And when finally he had his yellow turnip blown off, he tucked it under his arm and snapped to attention –'

'Where his severed head yelled Heil Hitler before he keeled over and fell dead, the sole victor.'

'Come, you, hero, do you want to live for ever?'

But the Butcher was not to be persuaded. 'Yer can talk till yer rupture yerselves,' he said. 'But I'm not going to release those shitting Mark IVs till I get a direct order from the CO – and that's that!'

Thus in the end they were forced to give up. Schulze looked at Matz. 'It's no go, Matzi. Let's get out of here before the yellow bastard gases us with all that green smoke he's making.'

As they retreated from the latrine, Schulze stopped and looked up the coast. The sun was already beginning to rise, flushing the sky a warm pink. Against it, two columns of black smoke rose lazily into the still air above Belleville. Beyond it, out to sea, he could just make out the hazy dark shapes of warships. It was obvious that the Tommies were landing in force and that the Wotan hadn't reached the Battery yet. 'Listen Matzi,' he said, 'you know how Goethe defined rape?'

'Eh?'

'Woman with skirt up can run faster than man with trousers down.'

'Did Goethe say that?'

'No, of course he didn't, you stupid little monkey's turd!'

110

'Well, why mention it then?'

'Because it proves a point.'

Matz shook his head. 'You know sometimes Schulze I think you've got a little bird up here,' he tapped his temple, 'which goes twit-twit all the time.'

Schulze ignored him. 'See here, if we took over those wet-tails and the Mark IVs, who's there to stop us?'

'The Butcher.'

'Right and where's the Butcher now?'

'He's making green smoke on his thunderbox.'

'So, how fast is he going to run with his knickers around his ankles? Get me, dummy?'

Matz's wrinkled face broke into an evil smile. He winked conspiratorially. 'Get you. Well, come on, what are you waiting for, you big Hamburg dum-dum!'

Hurriedly they crossed to where the five Mark IVs were buried beneath their mass of camouflage, sole survivors of the thirty odd with which they entered the fighting in Russia that spring. Around them their youthful, black-clad crews stared, half in fear and half in eagerness to get into action, at the armada slowly emerging from the haze above the sea.

'Pay attention, you bunch of aspagarus Tarzans, I want to talk to you!' bellowed Schulze above the noise.

The youths turned round curiously, staring down from the tanks' camouflaged decks at the two NCOs, the one with his wooden leg, the other with two monstrously wrinkled white hands. 'You all know me, I'm Schulze, the First Company's pox-cop.'

There were a few hesitant laughs.

'That's right,' Schulze urged, 'get it off yer consumptive little chests, because it'll be the last laugh you'll get this day! Now all of you are shitty wet-tailed greenbacks, although you might think you're soldiers take it from an old head like me, you ain't. But this day I'm going to do you a favour. Your days of being Christmas Tree soldiers are over.' He poked a hideously white thumb at his broad chest heavy with the decorations of three years war, 'Sergeant Schulze is going to turn you into real soldiers – for nothing.'

The laughs were fewer this time. But Schulze was pleased to see the look of eager determination in the young men's eyes.

'Now you can drive and you fire a 75mm – that's all. You know nothing about tank tactics or how to fight a Mark IV. Let us understand that right from the start. Matz here is going to give you the short course, aren't you, Corporal?'

Matz didn't hesitate. He limped forward and pushed aside his big crony. 'All right, wet-tails, I'm going to tell you this one time and one time only. The second time, you'll be dead, looking at the potatoes from beneath. So get it! In the kind of street-fighting against infantry we're going into, there are three things to remember. One, keep the arse of yer Mark IV covered all the time, otherwise some nasty Tommy's gonna stick a bazooka round up it – without the vaseline. Two,' he ticked the point on his dirty fingers. 'Keep correct road distance – two hundred metres is best. So if the feller at the point buys it, you can still bug out – er, execute a tactical retreat. Thirdly,' Matz rolled his evil little eyes around, taking in their tense smooth faces, wondering just how many of these innocents would survive the day, 'watch the road verges on the roads around here. They'll give way just like that,' he clicked his fingers sharply, 'under the weight of your Mark IV. And a bunch of dum-dums like you wouldn't have a hope in hell of getting out again. You'd be sitting ducks for the Tommy infantry – and they'd just love to toast your eggs with one of those flame-throwers of theirs till they're nice and crisp and as black as Satan's arse!'

'All right,' Schulze broke in. 'That's enough of the short course, Corporal Matz, we don't want these nice lads wetting their knickers before they've even seen a Tommy, do we?'

He looked up at the blond, hard-jawed young lance-corporal standing on the deck of the nearest Mark IV. 'You, laddie. I'm

112

going to take your tank as my command tank. Clear?'

'Clear, sir!' the boy sprang to attention as if he were speaking to the Vulture himself.

'The rest of you will proceed up the road to Belleville at the distance Corporal Matz proscribed. Gunners watch out for Tommies in the field. If you see one of them carrying a long blunt thing, it won't be his erection or his box of sandwiches, it'll be a bazooka. Don't hesitate, knock the bastard out before he screws you. I shall take my command vehicle and try to guard the right flank. That's the one closest to the sea, the way the Tommies are going to come in. The ground's dicey, but I'm relying on the talents of Corporal Matz, cripple though he is, to get us through safely. If he don't,' he added threateningly, 'I'm going to hand him over personally to the Tommies and let them have a dose of him – I've had enough ... Once we hit the village, I'll request infantry cover from the rest of the Battalion and then we'll go in and really give those Tommies a nasty swift kick up their skinny, tea-drinking asses. Clear?'

'Clear, Sergeant!' they bellowed back.

Schulze looked at them for a moment as they stood there above him, silhouetted against the blood-red rays of the rising sun and his face softened. 'Don't worry, lads, old Schulze won't let you down,' he said. Then his voice hardened again. 'All right mount up!' he bellowed.

They scrambled into their vehicles, gunners and drivers sliding hastily into their separate hatches. On the turrets the commanders slipped into their earphones. Schulze pushed past the lance-corporal. Below Matz pressed the red button. The tank's 400hp engines coughed throatily like a heavy smoker on a cold morning. Nothing. He pressed the button again. A faint whirr. Something stirred behind. 'Come on, Matzi,' Schulze bellowed impatiently. 'The Tommies'll be back in England for tea by the time you get shitting well started!' Matz stabbed the button for a third time. Suddenly the great engines sprang

113

into noisy life and the whole massive metal monster shook wildly. Matz gunned the engines. Schulze quickly checked the line to see if everybody had started up. Then he waved his hand round his head and pointed forward. *'Roll 'em, my lucky lads,'* he yelled above the tremendous racket. *'We're going to pay the English gentlemen a visit!'*

Behind them, Sergeant Major Metzger staggered out of the latrine holding up his unbuttoned trousers with both hands. 'Stop,' he cried desperately, 'you can't shitting well go off like that.'

He attempted to run forward to stop Schulze. But his pants dropped to his knees. He staggered, tried to prevent himself from falling but sprawled full length in the dust, his trousers around his knees, his massive bottom thrust towards the sky.

'Will wonders never cease?' a happy Schulze laughed, 'the moon has risen already!'

FIVE

'Awfully nice of the old Hun, what, sir,' Freddy remarked airily, surveying the gully packed five foot deep with wire which led up the cliff from the shore. 'Weally makes a chap feel welcome.'

'Yer ain't bloodily well kidding, Freddy,' returned the Laird, taking in the scene on the lonely, still beach. A haze of mist and smoke had drifted across the sea behind them. Nevertheless it was clear that theirs was the only Eureka of the 7th Commando's force which had survived the E-boat attack. Nearly four hundred of his men had bought it within a matter of minutes, dead or drowned even before they had had a chance to have a go at the Jerries.

'Well, Freddy,' the Colonel concluded, 'it looks as if at least the buggers haven't spotted us.'

The tall Scots Guards' officer nodded. 'But somebody's getting a bit of a pasting not far off.' He swept his cane in the direction from which the persistent crackle of small arms fire was coming.

'That'll be the lads of the Froggie Resistance – the op Lord Louis laid on for us. All right, let's get down to cases.' He swung round to the men crouched in a semi-circle around him in the wet sand, weapons at the alert, their craggy, long Highland faces tense but determined. 'Look lads, I won't joss yer, we're right up the proverbial creek without a sodding paddle. But we've been in worse fixes than this before. Think of the ruddy ballsup at Vaagso for example.'

'Ay, ay, yer right there, Laird,' came the rumble of agreement from the men.

The little CO breathed a sigh of relief and thanked God for

the steadiness of his Jocks; cockneys from the Big Smoke would have reacted a lot differently. 'Okay, lads, we're gonna have a bash at that Battery. There are only eighteen of us and I don't think we can take the ruddy place as originally planned. But I *do* think we can have a bloody good try at harassing them.' He looked carefully round at their red Highland faces, the product of years of open-air life. 'I know what yer all thinking,' he said carefully. 'Yer thinking we're not gonna get out of this mess alive, eh?'

The men lowered their eyes, and he said hurriedly. 'I can't guarantee nothing. But I'll tell you this, the Canucks depend on us and if we don't pull it off, well we've still got snotty here to take us away in his little sailboat. Haven't we Snotty?'

'Right, sir – I mean ay, ay, sir,' replied the boy Lieutenant.

'There you are,' the Laird beamed at his men. 'If a little un like that, snatched from the cradle by Winnie, and a Sassenach to boot, is ready to have a go, what have a lot of hairy-arsed old Jocks like us got to fear! All right on yer plates o' meat and follow me!'

Without any further ado he slung his rifle more comfortably on his shoulder, hitched up his bedraggled kilt and grasped the first string of wire held by two metal pegs driven deep into the white cliff. The prongs dug cruelly into his palm. But he repressed his cry of pain. The wire was completely taut and hardly gave at all when he put his full weight on it. 'Trust old Jerry,' he said through gritted teeth. 'When he does a job o' work, he does it thorough. We can walk up this sodding stuff like a ladder, courtesy of old Hitler.

'All right, Freddy, you bring up the rear, the rest will follow. If any squarehead shows his head above the top of the cliff, you've my permission to shoot the bugger.'

'Thank you, sir.'

'But what about me? Can't I go along, sir?' It was the Navy sub-lieutenant. He looked pleadingly at the little CO.

'Better leave it to us brown jobs, we've been trained for it,'

116

the Laird began, then he changed his mind. 'All right, laddie, come along, if you want and earn yersel the sodding Victoria Cross.'

The climb was hell. With not a pair of wire cutters among the lot of them they were stopped time and time again by cunningly constructed wire ledgers which the Germans had designed specifically to stop such an effort as theirs. Each time the Laird, hanging on with one lacerated hand, the blood pouring down his wrist, used his free hand to throw a toggle rope up and over it. Then when it had caught there, he launched himself into space, his kilt flying wildly. As he came down again, he crashed his heavy boots against the wire barrier and wedged thus, continued the climb, heart beating like a triphammer, up to the next clear strand of wire.

To the Laird it seemed as though the noise they made should have woken the Germans as far away as Berlin, and struggling painfully through the wire, he felt like one of his favourite winkles stuck on the end of a pin, at the mercy of enemy snipers.

But at last he reached the top, and for a moment he crouched there, his kilt in tatters, his hands and bare knees cut to ribbons, his lungs wheezing like a pair of broken bellows. Then he pulled himself together and raised his head cautiously above the edge of the cliff.

To his right lay the village of Berneval shrouded in smoke, split here, there and everywhere by the scarlet muzzle flashes of riflefire. Then came a small stretch of woodland, approaching close to the Battery. He recognised it immediately from the hours he had spent studying it on the sand-table in training. Each of the machine-gun pits was clearly outlined against the crimson sky, while beyond he could see tiny black figures on the gun turrets with their binoculars trained on the sea, waiting for the fleet to come within range so that they could open fire and destroy it.

'Hell!' the Laird cursed as the next man came to a gasping

halt beneath him. He knew they couldn't hang on the cliff very long without being spotted. But how were they going to get over the top into the cover of the wood without being seen by one of the observers on the gun turrets?

It was just then that the survivors of the ill-fated Seventh Commando struck lucky for the first time since they had left England.

The first flight of twin-engined Bostons came barrelling in at 300 mph from the sea. Engines howling, tearing the silence apart, they swooped over the coast at tree-top level. The shallow curve of the bay erupted into a hell of fire. At the battery, the multiple flak chattered crazily. Red, white and green tracer zipped through the pink sky. The first Boston released its bombs. The Laird had no time to see whether they found their target. The air attack was the cover he needed.

'Pass the word down,' he yelled the clatter of the flak and the staccato rattle of the heavy ack-ack machine-guns which sounded like a walking stick being drawn across railings, 'as soon as you get to the top, make a run for the wood. All right, here I go!'

Grabbing his rifle and hitching his kilt above his knees, the Laird burst across the top of the cliff and set off in wild dash for the cover of the pines. Another squadron of Bostons hurtled across the coast. The flak gunners swung round with the multiple cannon. The air was full of flying steel, as they pounded away. But the Laird ran on, unobserved, twisting and turning to avoid the shrapnel flying everywhere, pelting his way furiously towards the cover of the trees, followed by a sergeant and one other man. They doubled across the cliff top to the wood.

The Laird flung himself full length into the undergrowth, ignoring the twigs tearing cruelly at his body. With a gasp of relief, he buried his burning, sweat-lathered face into the still damp ground. Man after man crashed into the trees all around him, burrowing their way out of sight as they had been trained to do. The Laird did not raise his head to check them. He was too exhausted from the climb up the cliff and the race across to the wood. Then Freddy's voice, a little less serene than usual, remarked. 'It appears we've done it, sir, without being spotted, what?'

The Laird forced himself up by a sheer effort of will and gasped. 'Good, lads ... very good.' He wiped a bloody hand across his sweat-lathered brow and looked at the crimson faces. 'First round to us, lads. Now, me band of brothers, into the breach once more, as the Immoral Bard says. Lads, we've got to improvise from now onwards. We can harass the buggers very effectively, if we can nab those mg posts there – there and there.' His finger trembled as he indicated the three machine-gun nests to the nearside of the Battery. 'With a bit of luck the Froggies will hold off the Jerries behind us, so all we've got to contend with – once we got the mg posts – is the guns and gunners themselves.' He sniffed contemptuously. 'And we all know what a pregnant duck yer average artilleryman is, don't we?'

There was a soft chorus of 'ays' from the men.

'Bloody lot of soft Nellies who wear pyjamas in bed, everybody knows that. We'll divide into three groups of six – you'll come with me Snotty, as second-in-command. Once we're out of these trees we've got to cover about two hundred yards of open ground before we hit the mg pits on this side.

'Freddy you take group one. Sergeant Gillies,' he turned to the elderly NCO who had once been his chief-gilly, 'you take number two and remember to keep that red, whisky-drinking conk of yourn down – it'll light us up otherwise like a ruddy beacon.'

The men laughed while Sergeant Gillies said seriously, 'Ah'll bear that in mind, Laird.'

'I'll take the third group. Now we crawl the whole way there and woe betide any of you buggers that lets himself get spotted before we get in close. I'll have him on a charge once

119

we're back in the UK quicker than lightning. Once we're in position, I'll give one blast on my whistle and then we go in with,' he hesitated for a moment while he fumbled with his skean dhu, 'with the cold steel!'

Behind him the young sailor shivered.

'Here come the Brylcreem boys again!' one of the men called as another flight came winging their way in at tree-top height, flak exploded in harsh red and yellow balls all around them.

The Laird did not hesitate. 'Come on, lads, spread out and let's go.' He winked at Freddy and his mouth formed the soundless words, 'best of luck, you long streak of piss!'

Freddy grinned, then they burst through the trees, the noise they made covered by the tremendous roar of the planes' engines as they began their long crawl towards the unsuspecting mg nests.

*   *   *

'Freeze!' ordered the Laird.

The handful of men sprawled in the scrub all around him stopped.

'What is it, sir?' the Snotty asked fearfully.

'Wire.'

'But we've no cutters.'

The Laird ignored him. 'Curtis and Menzies,' he ordered.

The two privates crawled forward hurriedly. Without a further order, they squirmed on their back in the short wet grass and seizing the lowest strand of wire in their horny hands, took the strain. Under their combined efforts they managed to raise it a foot or so off the ground, the sweat streaming down their faces.

'All right, here, I come.' The Colonel crawled swiftly forward, carefully dragging his skinny body through so that his tattered kilt did not catch on a strand. 'Now Collins and Mackenzie.'

The two commandos followed him and took the strain from their comrades. One by one the others followed and grouped around their CO. He nodded, satisfied. 'Good lads. All right, now lower it nice and gentle. We don't want to set off no Jerry booby traps.'

They were less than twenty-five yards away from their objective now. They could hear the excited chatter of the mg crew quite clearly during the breaks in firing. Cautiously the Laird took out his skean dhu and raised his head. He could count four Jerries in their coal-scuttle helmets. 'Four of 'em,' he whispered. 'By Christ we outnumber them!'

'All right, spread out; you four take the left. Me and this high ranking naval person will take the right. Once I see you're within five yards of the buggers, I'll blow me penny whistle. Off you go.'

Obediently the four privates began to crawl rapidly to the left. The Laird looked at the pale-faced Snotty and winked. 'Don't worry, lad, it'll be just like in the pictures. Come on.' Swiftly he squirmed forward, his kilted rump moving rhythmically from side to side just in front of the Snotty's nose, skean dhu clenched between his teeth. He could now smell the Germans, that peculiar odour of German serge uniform cloth and the hard ersatz wartime soap which he had come to know in the last few terrible years. Sending a hasty prayer winging its way to heaven that the other groups were already in position, he transferred the evil little knife to his right hand and thrust his whistle into his mouth. He took a deep breath and blew.

The scream of hoarse Scots rage was followed an instant later by a cry of alarm, as the dust-stained, ragged, bleeding figures of the commandos burst into view.

A German tried to swing the gun round, his face frantic with sudden fear. Curtis disobeyed orders and shot him from the hip. He went down screaming, sprawling over his spandau. The Laird dived at the man trying to take his place, ripping open his stomach.

Next to him the Snotty was on the floor of the gunpit, trying to fight off a furious, red-faced gunner who was smashing his ham of a fist into the sailor's face over and over again.

The Laird sprang on to the cursing German's back like a tartan-clad monkey. With one hand he grabbed the man's helmet, with the other, slashed his razor-sharp knife across the exposed white flesh of his throat.

Precisely one minute later the last gunner lay sprawled out dead at the bottom of the pit, a bayonet thrust through his chest. Five minutes later, while the boy sobbed gently next to the body of the dead gunner, Freddy dropped into the pit, minus his stocking cap, but otherwise as imperturbable as ever to report, 'We've got them, sir – the other two and what do you think we found in my pit?'

'Shirley Temple?' the Laird ventured, highly pleased with the success of his operation and wiping the blood off the skean dhu on his kilt.

'No, a thwee inch gun mortar. Wipping, what, sir!'

'*Wipping*, Freddy!' the Laird exclaimed, his heart leaping.

They were really in business. Not only had they three German machine-guns at their disposal, but also a mortar. Its bombs would probably bounce off the thick concrete of the turrets like pingpong balls, but it would make the Jerries sit up and take notice.

'Any casualties?'

'Not a one. Though I'm definitely not wegimental without my cap, sir.'

The Laird of Abernockie and Dearth grinned. 'Silly old sod,' he muttered affectionately. 'All right, Freddy, nip back to your lot and tell Sergeant Gillies on the way, this is what we gonna do. I'll give you two minutes to clean these stiffs out and set yourselves up and then we're gonna let the Jerries have all we've got, aiming at the firing slits and air vents wherever possible. By Christ, Freddy you old fart, those buggers over

122

there are going to think that the whole Seventh Commando has suddenly opened up behind them! Before this day is over, Freddy, a lot of them lads behind that concrete are going to be wetting their knickers good and proper.'

SIX

The squat shape of the lead tank, outlined clearly on the raised coastal road, rumbled towards the embattled village of Belleville. The other three Mark IVs followed, spaced out at regular intervals as Matz had ordered, their 75mm guns swinging from side to side like the snouts of predatory monsters searching for prey.

Watching their progress from the flank, Schulze nodded his approval. He pressed his throat mike and asked: 'How's it going down there, Matzi?'

'Dicey,' Matz's voice came from the driver's seat strangely unreal and distorted over the intercom, 'there's patches of shitty salt marsh everywhere. Miss one and we'd be up to the boogies in mud.'

'Tough tittie,' Schulze answered unsympathetically. 'But keep up the good work. I'll see you get the War Service Cross, fourth class for this.'

Matz buried in the belly of the tank, muttered a gross obscenity.

'Yes and *your* mother too!' Schulze replied and released the pressure on his throat mike. 'Corporal,' he snapped at the hard-faced boy next to him.

'Sir!'

'Keep your eyes on that ground ahead. If you see anything that looks like marsh grass, sing out fast.'

'Sir!'

Schulze sniffed and turned his attention to the smoke-shrouded village a kilometre or so away. He bit his bottom lip anxiously. There was no doubt about it. He could make out both the high-pitched hiss of the SS assault rifle and the slower chatter of what must be Tommy weapons. Wotan was in action up there and by the sound of it the Tommies had them by the short and curlies.

He dismissed the worrying thought from his mind and concentrated on the problem of how he was going to get his little command with its raw unskilled crews into action. Once they reached the village, he decided, he'd let them try a dash down the main street, while he swung round behind the village with his command tank. With a bit of luck he'd pull it off. Infantry was usually shit-scared of armour, especially if it were moving fast. The only problem would be if the Tommies had bazookas. Then they would be sitting ducks in the tight village street with no room to manoeuvre.

'Sir!' the Corporal's voice broke urgently into his thoughts.

'What?' Schulze swung round. The boy was staring at the dark shape of a man which had risen from the long parched grass at the side of the road just behind the lead tank. He had a strange bell-shaped object in his hand.

'What do you make of it, sir? What is it –'

'Get your shitty body down inside the turret!' Schulze cried and pushed him down. As the man started to run forward to the rear of the slowly moving Mark IV, Schulze whirled the 10-ton turret round. At the same time he swung up the turret machine-gun, ready to go into action immediately, and fumbled feverishly until he had the running man in his sights, bisected neatly by the metal bar. He squeezed the trigger. Four hundred metres away, the running man stopped in mid-stride, his spine arched, his hands raised, as though he were appealing to the heavens for mercy. Then the bell-shaped object tumbled from his nerveless fingers and he pitched forward to lie still in the grass.

Schulze breathed out hard, 'Christ on a crutch, that was close!'

'What was it, sir?'

'Sticky bomb. Held by magnet and –' He broke off sud-

125

denly. Another tiny figure had sprung up from the grass and was racing up the road after the tank with a bomb in his hand.

'A suicide squad!' Schulze yelled, and grabbed the mg to fire another burst. The first man hit the road, his back torn open. But just as Schulze's slugs scythed through his legs, the leading soldier managed to attach the grenade to the rear of the unsuspecting Mark IV. Even at that distance they could hear the hollow clang as the magnets gripped.

'Holy strawsack,' Schulze groaned. 'Wake up you shitty dum-dums, don't yer know you've got a cuckoo up yer arse.'

The Mark IV rolled on, leaving the dying man behind it, until suddenly there was a thick asthmatic explosion, and it reared up on its back sprockets like a bucking horse. As it crashed down again it began to burn fiercely.

'Get out! Oh, come on, get out!' Schulze cried despairingly, hammering his white fist on the side of the turret. 'Make it, lads!'

But no one emerged from the stricken tank and suddenly the air was full of the sweet stench of burning flesh. The young corporal next to Schulze began to vomit over the side of the turret.

There was no time to concern himself now with the fate of the lead tank's crew, for two hundred metres behind it, the second Mark IV had come to a halt, its commander obviously at a loss to know what to do. Schulze grabbed for the throat mike. 'Reverse, you son of a whore!' he yelled urgently. '*Reverse.*' But the tank commander had obviously not got his set tuned to receive. He couldn't hear. Panicked by the fate of the lead tank, exposed as it had been on the elevated road, he decided to get into the grass.

'No!' Schulze cried in despair. '*No!*'

But the tank commander could not hear his desperate cry and his driver began cautiously to edge his thirty-ton monster over the steep verge. Almost immediately what Matz had pre-

126

dicted happened and the verge began to crumble. A horrified Schulze could clearly see the sandy soil start to yield. Frantically, the driver revved his engine, trying to keep the tank from slipping more, but slowly and inevitably the Mark IV began to slide into the ditch.

The enemy suicide squad did not need a second invitation. Covered from Schulze's fire by the stricken monster's bulk, they swarmed forward to attach their deadly bombs to its sides.

Further down the road the gunner of number three tank tried to swat them off the Mark IV's deck. Man after man fell, but they were invincible. A moment later the Mark IV in the ditch was torn apart. Its ten-ton turret sailed high into the air. Its tracer ammunition zig-zagged crazily in all directions. A crewman tumbled out of the wreckage and attempted to walk on bloody stumps towards number three tank, but a blast of shotgun fire caught him before he had staggered ten paces.

Schulze pressed his throat-mike. 'Back off, you stupid sods!' He roared. 'Back off right away!'

This time the tank commander received Schulze's message and his driver started to reverse up the road while the commander covered their retreat with smoke grenades.

'Good ... that's it,' Schulze chuckled. 'You and your comrade back right up to those trees ... that's the way ... Once you get there, everyone on deck with his weapons right to tackle any more of those shitty suicide squads ... Keep radio watch and I'll call you up as soon as the road is clear ... Over and out!' He released his pressure on the mike.

'All right, what now, Colonel Schulze?' Matz's voice came up from below. 'Go on giving orders like that and you'll be able to take over from the Vulture soon.'

'Aw, go and piss in yer dice-beaker,' Schulze snarled. 'You've got to give those shitty greenbeaks orders like that.'

'Yer'll be powdering their sweet little baby popos next, Schulze!'

'Stick yer prick up yer arse and give yersen a cheap thrill,' Schulze snorted. But his heart wasn't in their usual repartee; he knew the Battalion needed the surviving tanks if they were going to break loose from the village. But the two tanks now hidden in the trees would never cover the last kilometre to the embattled village as long as there were still suicide squads out there in the ditches. They would have to be flushed out first and it was up to him to do it.

'Listen Matz,' he said, 'do you think you could cross that road?'

'With my eyes closed.'

'Those verges are tricky.'

'Little fish!' Matz said contemptuously. 'Didn't I get through the Perekop Isthmus* with my boogies up to the top in mud all right?'

'All right, all right. Don't have an orgasm! We all know you're the best driver Wotan has. Now this is what I'm gonna do. We'll cut the road five hundred metres further on. I hope those bastards of the suicide squad will think we're beating it. Then we'll come back and roll'em up. And you know what I mean, Matzi, don't you?'

Matz did. Wherever the suicide squad men had dug themselves in, they would crush them to death by whirling round and round until the sides of the hole yielded and the whole weight of the tank descended upon the unfortunate men huddled below.

'Hey,' he protested, 'we might land ourselves in the shit there. If we start doing our little *pas de deux* in marshy ground we could find ourselves sinking in deeper than we wanted.'

'I know, you little currant-crapper, I've thought of that one too. This is what we're going to do . . .'

*   *   *

* See Leo Kessler *Death's Head*.

Schulze dropped the wooden mallet, satisfied with the job he had done on the twin exhaust pipes. 'All right,' he nodded to the lance-corporal who had been guarding him with his machine-pistol. 'Tell Matz to start up again!'

The boy shouted something inside the turret. Matz pressed the starter button. The great engines sprang to life at once. The little one-legged driver gunned the motors. Thick streams of choking blue smoke gushed downwards as Schulze had planned they would.

'Tell him, it's working,' he yelled at the boy above the roar of the engines.

'What's it for, sir?'

'You'll see, lad, you'll see in due course. Now you watch the rear of this here battle wagon and I'll take the front. If any of those bastards show themselves with those shitty bombs, shoot to kill. Clear?'

'Clear, sir.'

Schulze knew that everything depended upon Matz. One false gear, one moment of hesitation, one miscalculation with the speed, and they would be crippled just as the second Mark IV had been.

Matz took his time, rolling forward at fifteen kilometres an hour, one eye on the ground ahead and one on the verges, looking for the most favourable spot to move on to the road. Three hundred metres ... four hundred ... five hundred metres. Then Matz spotted it. A slight indentation in the side of the road which might well give him some sort of purchase.

Matz licked dry lips and eyed the spot carefully. He would have to go at it fairly quickly, then when he was half way up, he would have to double-declutch as quick as hell, bring the gear lever right across the gate and finish the last bit in low gear. Once on the road, he'd then have to rev up, flash through the twenty odd gears of the Mark IV and take her down the other side at speed before the loose soft earth of the verge crumbled beneath the tank.

'Schulze?' he called.

'Yes, monkey's turd.'

'I'm going up over there – at two o'clock. You see that hole in the road?'

'Got it!'

'All right, then hold tight. Here we go!' Matz rammed home high gear and revved the engine. The tank started to increase speed, its deck vibrating wildly. On top the young corporal and Schulze grabbed for a hand hole and watched the verge.

'If you believe in the Big Man up there in a white shirt sitting on a cloud, you'd better start praying, son,' Schulze cracked, but there was no warmth in his eyes; he knew what would happen to them if Matz failed to make it. The tank hit the verge. The gear lever shook crazily as the tracks took the slope. It rose and seemed to fill the whole driving compartment. With a quick, impatient gesture, Matz wiped the sweat off his brow and slowly counted five. The engine sounded as if it were on its last legs. Matz lunged forward and grabbed the lever with a hand that was soaked with sweat. Then he crashed the great metal clutch down hard, once, twice. With a grunt he threw the gear lever right across the bar into bottom gear.

For one frightening moment nothing happened. The tank seemed to teeter there, and he could hear nothing except his own harsh anxious breathing. Then all at once the engine broke into its full-throated roar and the tracks began to grip. He had traction. She was going up.

'That's the way, you son-of-bitch,' he cried enthusiastically, a huge grin over his wrinkled face. 'Come on, take it ... take it!'

The Mark IV lurched over the edge of the road. Matz changed up, sliding effortlessly through the tank's score of gears, simultaneously crashing his foot down hard on the accelerator. As it shot forward a machine-gun opened up somewhere. Slugs pattered against the metal sides, but Matz had no ears for them.

'That's it, you son-of-bitch,' he yelled, recognising the right note immediately. 'Here we go – and you'd better get us down right, or you'll have the toe of my dicebeaker up your beautiful tin arse!'

The Mark IV lurched forward alarmingly. The gear lever began to tremble violently once again. An anxious sweat bathed Matz's body and soaked his shirt black. A thrill of fear went through him, for the tank was beginning to slide. He could feel the see-sawing motion and knew that he was losing traction.

'*Whore!*' he screamed. 'Shitting, slack-cunted bitch of a whore ... please, please *come*!'

Almost delicately, he eased the right tiller bar back like a doctor touching a woman's breast. Outside he could hear the right track begin to whirl aimlessly and realised that they were definitely slipping.

Mouthing terrible obscenities, Matz continued his delicate pressure on the rod which braked the track and enabled the tank to swing to left or right. Still nothing happened. He eased his foot off the clutch. It was a dangerous move that could bring disaster. But he was not going to allow himself to slide into the ditch without a fight. He exerted a little more pressure on the tiller bar.

It seemed like a miracle when the tank responded, and the right track braked and started to grip again. Matz released the pressure immediately and the Mark IV rolled forward in a straight course, taking the rest of the verge easily.

'What the hell were you doing down there just then, you shitty cripple,' Schulze's voice flooded his ears. 'You've gone and made me wet me skivvies! And laddo next to me is giving off green smoke.'

'Aw, go and piss up your sleeve,' Matz snarled, as he

rammed home a higher gear and they rumbled forward once more.

They took the first hole without any trouble. Instead of breaking for safety, the suicide squad men decided to stay where they were and let the tank roll over them. It was standard operating procedure, but they didn't know the veterans of Wotan, trained in the brutal, merciless fighting of the Eastern Front. Instead of just rolling over the hole, Matz jerked back his left tiller bar and swung the tank round right on the edge of the cunningly concealed dug-out. He could imagine what the men below him were feeling, their lungs filled with the stench of diesel, their eardrums threatening to burst with the roar, faces seared by the heat from the exhausts, eyes closed like children. But there was no room for mercy. He swung the big tank round once again and the side of the pit started to crumble, eventually giving way altogether. The Mark IV lurched to one side, its tracks still running, churning the bodies of the men below into a bloody pulp.

A group of *Maquis* tried to make a break for it. Schulze's machine gun chattered. Remorsely the metal monster rumbled over their twitching bodies.

'Look out!' Matz shouted a sudden warning.

'What is it, Matzi?'

'Soft stuff ahead. Three o'clock next to the tree – and there's a hole with Frogs in it right in the middle.'

'Got it, Matzi,' Schulze answered, identifying the pit in the middle of the marshy grass. 'I'll leave it to you. Let's give the murderous bastards a taste of our special stuff.'

Cautiously Matz drove the tank towards the hole. The ashen-faced men, sensing the terrible death that lay ahead for them, poured a furious hail of fire at the tank. Schulze and the corporal ducked behind the turret and listened to the slugs career off the Mark IV's thick armour. The firing stopped. The terrified Frenchmen ducked, for the monster was almost upon them, its squat metal shape blotting out the blood-red sun, filling the whole world, throwing everything into a hot, diesel-stinking darkness.

Carefully Matz positioned his tank above the hole. But this time he did not hurl the vehicle round and round in fury until the sides of the pit caved in. Instead, making sure that his tracks were resting on firm ground, he took his foot off the clutch and began to rev the engine.

'What's he doing, sir?' asked the corporal curiously.

'You a country-boy?'

'Yes, from Bavaria.'

'What do you do then, hayseed, when you want to get rid of rats in the farmyard?' Schulze snapped, as Matz raced his engines louder.

'You gas them, sir.'

'Yes,' Schulze said, his face grim at the thought of what was happening to the men below.

'*Jesus, Maria, Joseph!*' the boy gasped, crossing himself in the Bavarian fashion as he realised why Schulze had hammered the exhausts downwards.

Five minutes later they had cleared the last pit in the same fashion, leaving the Maquis in it sprawled out in the gestures of mortally terrified men, their hands turned to claws of fear, their faces green, their mouths filled with vomit, and were signalling the two tanks hidden in the trees that the road to Belleville was clear at last!

'What now, sir?' the corporal asked, not daring to look back at the men who had died so horribly.

'We're not risking the road again and those verges,' Schulze said firmly. 'We'll leave that to the other two.' He surveyed the smoke-shrouded village with narrowed eyes. 'You see that track up there?'

'Yessir.'

'We'll make for that. It looks as if it'll get on to the parallel road to the main road.'

'And then, sir?'

'Then, laddie,' Schulze answered with more confidence than he felt, 'we looks for Major von Dodenburg and those wet-tails of the First Company!'

SEVEN

Major von Dodenburg, helmetless, his face streaked with sweat and dirt, raged inwardly. Half his company of Hitler Youth volunteers lay sprawled dead on the bloody cobbles outside; his contact with the Vulture, wherever he might be, was completely cut off, and the shaken, scared survivors of his Company dared not even venture into the centre of ground floors to which they clung with desperate tenacity lest a Maquis shot them through the thinly plastered ceiling.

Von Dodenburg cast around desperately for some way out, his back pressed against the dirty kitchen wall. It was no use attempting to assault the primitive wooden stairs that led to the upper floor packed with Maquis gunmen. These were barricaded and they would have been shot down mercilessly before they had set foot on the first rung. Nor was it any good attempting the street again. At periodic intervals the Maquis swept it with their English machine-guns and any attempt at a breakout would have attracted the whole weight of the enemy fire.

In the end von Dodenburg realised that there was only one way out of the trap in which they found themselves: they would have to apply the standard street-fighting procedure, despite the fact that his handful of scared survivors were completely untrained in the technique.

He leaned forward and said more confidently than he felt, 'Now listen you Hitler Youth heroes, we're in a mess. But we can get out of it, if we keep our heads and move systematically. Do you understand?'

Hesitantly they nodded, the light of hope beginning to dawn in their eyes.

'We're in a house at the end of the row, and this wall behind me is not covered by any of the enemy. In essence it is in dead ground as far as they are concerned,' he lied hopefully. 'You get it?'

They nodded again.

'So we are going to use that dead ground to our advantage. We're going to burrow through that wall and if there are no windows to give us away on this side, we'll head for the roof. Once there, we'll take off a few tiles and work our way downwards again. Then the tables will be reversed—'

'And we'll be shitting on them and not them on us,' one boy interjected.

'Correct. And once we've got this place cleared of the rats, we'll move on to the roof of the next house and do the same thing all over again. It'll be a damn long-winded procedure, but there is no other way. Are you with me?'

'Yes, we're with you, sir,' came back the chorus of eager replies.

'All right, the men on this side of the wall get your entrenching tools out and start hacking away – here. You lot over there begin firing up into the ceiling to cover their noise. I don't want the Frogs to get wise to what we're about. Let them think they've got us nice and trapped down here until we're in position to give them the worse headache they've ever had in their lives.'

*   *   *

Von Dodenburg wriggled cautiously through the rubble and rose to his feet carefully, machine-pistol in hand. Behind him in the street the Maquis gunfire was still going on, but the alley in which he now found himself was silent and empty. He looked up at the side of the house and breathed a sigh of relief. It was bare of windows right up to the yellow leaves of tobacco hanging under the eaves to dry. Swiftly he slung his machine-pistol around his neck.

136

'As quietly as you can,' he whispered to the men waiting tensely behind him in the acrid, smoke-filled room, their shoulders covered with flakes of plaster from the bullet-riddled ceiling. 'I'm going up; you follow. Once we're up there, we're in business.'

Von Dodenburg stretched to his full height and caught hold of the edge of the blackened roof-beam which stuck through the whitened stone above his head. Hardly daring to breathe, he pulled himself upwards. For a moment he balanced, slim body pressed tight against the outer wall of the upper storey. Only the thin stone wall separated him from the Maquis. If they heard him now, nothing could stop their bullets from tearing his defenceless body to pieces.

He reached up once again, seized hold of the eaves. A piece of rotten wood gave way in his hand and for a moment he thought the whole structure was going to come apart. But then it held. Slowly he began to heave himself upwards. His nose filled with the bitter fragrance of the drying tobacco leaves and suddenly he was dragging himself up and over the eaves on to the tiles themselves.

For a moment he lay there on the warm tiles, catching his breath and listening keenly to discover if he had been spotted from below, then sat up, peeled off his boots and crept on stockinged feet to the chimney where he left them.

The first man had appeared over the edge of the eaves. Von Dodenburg helped him up and signed to him to remove his boots too.

As soon as there were four of them crouched on the red roof, von Dodenburg raised one of the red tiles and placed it carefully to one side. Together they peeled off the tiles until they had uncovered over a square metre of roof. The musty stench of a century of neglect rose to meet them.

Von Dodenburg wrinkled his nose disgustedly, and bending his head, peered carefully below. He could see the usual blackened roof joists and beams, and below them a thin plaster ceiling through which he glimpsed the thin strips of wood that supported the ceiling. They were old and brittle and he knew that a swift kick would send the whole ceiling crashing down.

He signalled the men to close up and whispered to one, 'Get your grenade. As soon as I kick a hole in that ceiling, lob it in. Then we all count to four and go in firing.' Von Dodenburg knew the danger of carrying out this type of operation with untrained men, but there was no other way. 'Make sure,' he added warningly, 'that we all go in back to back. That way,' he forced a smile, 'we kill the Frogs and not each other!'

'All right, stand back.' He rose to his full height and jabbed his stockinged heel through the lathes. They crumbled at once, almost dragging him with them. A jagged hole appeared. There was a surprised *'les Boches!'* from below. The boy dropped his stick grenade into the hole carefully. Together they counted four. Below the room was rent by a great explosion. A wave of blast slapped von Dodenburg in the face like a blow. A moment later all four of them dropped through the roof, firing wildly.

The interior of the upper room was an incredible shambles. Dead and dying Maquis lay groaning everywhere, caught completely by surprise. One of them tried to stagger to his feet, sten-gun in his bloody hands. With almost careless brutality von Dodenburg let him have the butt of his Schmeisser in the face. Next to him, the boy who had lobbed the grenade put his rifle to the base of the Frenchman's skull and pulled the trigger.

'All right, that's enough!' von Dodenburg ordered harshly turning over the body of the man nearest him with his toe. Most of the man's face had gone, torn off by the full force of the grenade. He was dead all right, as were the rest of the Frenchmen crumpled in the bloody mess. 'You,' von Dodenburg ordered the boy, 'get our boots down. The rest of you help to get rid of this barricade.' He bent down and grabbed at the heavy plank of wood wedged between an ancient farmer's chest, which had been used to bar the stairs. 'We want the rest of them up here at the double. We've got a damnably long job in front of us if we're ever going to clear this street and get to that battery!'

*   *   *

But von Dodenburg was mistaken. Ten minutes later, after having cleared the second house, as he was making a personal reconnaissance of the roof of the third house, he heard the unmistakable rattle of tank tracks. He raised himself carefully and peered over his shoulder. His heart leaped as he recognised the squat silhouette of the Mark IV and watched it making its way cautiously down a little track from the fields into the village. The Maquis had already spotted it and were directing a steady stream of tracer at it, but the bullets were bouncing off its thick armoured glacis plate as if they were ping-pong balls.

Von Dodenburg bit his bottom lip thoughtfully. Although the Mark IV was buttoned up for action and he couldn't see the crew, he knew instinctively that only two men could have managed to barrel through the *Maquis* traps set for the Germans on the coastal road – the big Hamburger Schulze and his little mate Matz. Von Dodenburg's dirt-streaked, bloody face lit up with a smile as if he had just spotted the whole weight of the Bodyguard Division with Sepp Dietrich in personal charge coming to their rescue.

Squirming round on to his back, he fumbled for his signal pistol. He loaded it swiftly and fired two hasty shots into the air. The first flare exploded and bathed the confused melee below a sickly green. An instant later there was a spurt of silver light as the second exploded. The Mark IV changed direction almost at once and von Dodenburg scuttled hastily for the safety of the second house as the angry Maquis fire turned on him, and the slugs whined off the tiles all around.

*   *   *

'It's the First!' Schulze cried excitedly, recognising von Dodenburg's green and white signal flares. 'Over there to the left!' He swung his machine-gun round and fired another short burst at the Maquis hidden in the sheds surrounding them.

'I know, I know,' Matz cried angrily, 'I'm not shitting well blind you know.' He pulled back the left tiller bar and jerked the Mark IV violently round, sending Schulze caareening against the hull. His mouth filled with salt-tasting blood.

'By the Great Whore of Buxtehude,' Schulze roared, 'watch what yer about, you perverted little banana sucker, or I'll rip off yer wooden leg and beat the porridge out of yer brains with it!'

Matz wasn't listening. Two hundred metres away a Maquis had flopped down directly in their path, a strange cumbersome object clasped to his shoulder. 'What's he up to, Schulze?' he cried.

'It's a Piat – a Tommy Piat!' Schulze yelled, recognising the primitive British bazooka immediately. 'If he gets that up our knickers, we won't be virgins any more!' Hastily he pressed the 75mm's pedal. The twin triangles of the sight met on the lone figure. He snatched at the firing lever. The 75mm erupted with a roar. The blast whipped back and filled the closed turret with hot acrid smoke. The HE* struck the ground just in front of the Piat-gunner. When the smoke had vanished, all that was left was a blackened, smoking hole in the ground where the gunner had been.

'What yer trying to do, Schulze,' Matz sneered, 'knocking out individual stubble-hoppers with a 75mm shell? Don't yer know those things cost twenty marks each?'

'Concentrate on pushing this pram or I'll stick the next one up your –' A group of Maquis burst from a shed, carrying sticky bombs. Schulze let them have a burst with his twin Spandaus. At 800 rounds a minute they didn't have a chance. A moment later the Mark IV rolled over them, its tracks cut-

* High explosive shell. (Transl.)

ting their bodies to pieces and flinging them out on either side like chopped beef.

Matz swung the tank into a parallel street and gasped, for it was littered with the bodies of the First Company; the dead in their camouflaged uniforms seemed to cover it like a crazily patterned carpet.

'Jesus, Maria, Joseph!' the corporal breathed. 'The First has caught a packet!'

Schulze nodded glumly, but then his face lit up. Fifty metres ahead of them a well-known figure had dropped from the second floor of the first house. It was von Dodenburg, gesturing wildly with his machine-pistol at the house.

Matz knew instinctively what he meant, revved up and crammed the gear lever across the bar. At thirty kilometres an hour, he crashed with full force into the ground floor. With bricks and beams raining down upon its turret and the plaster falling like heavy snow, the Mark IV came to a halt, its motor stalled and its long hooded gun poked menacingly through what was left of the window to the street.

'In three devils' name, am I glad to see you!' von Dodenburg exclaimed as Matz and Schulze threw open their separate hatches.

'Got yerself in a nice old mess without us, haven't you, sir?' Schulze said. 'Some people oughtn't to be allowed out on their own.'

'Very true, very true,' von Dodenburg said, then his grin of welcome vanished. 'We've got ourselves in a nasty mess. You're going to have to take out each second floor along the other side of the street – and be careful, our boys are in most of the houses too, on the bottom floor.'

'Be as easy as pissing in a pail!' Schulze said confidently and swung himself behind the big 75mm again. 'All right, Frogs,' he roared as the corporal thrust home the first shell, 'prepare to go to your sodding heaven!'

'And hurry it up,' von Dodenburg yelled, as Schulze swung

the turret round. 'I want this damn street cleared in thirty minutes!'

The great gun drowned his words as it roared into violent life. The first shell hissed flatly through the air and hit the farthest house with a satisfying crack. As the wall blew apart and the Maquis men stumbled into the street, they were mown down by the automatics of the waiting SS men, eager for revenge.

Fifteen minutes later, Schulze popped his head out of the turret, sweat streaming down his grinning face and gave von Dodenburg a comic parody of a salute. 'Have I the Major's permission to report that the street is cleared?'

'Fuck off!' said von Dodenburg before the survivors were surging forward behind the cover of the lone tank. The road to the Goebbels Battery was open again.

EIGHT

It was furnace hot now. Above the still sea the sky was the colour of smoke through which the sun glittered like a copper coin.

On the broad sea front the German infantry waited, listening to the roar and snarl of the enemy planes, their gaze concentrated ahead, knowing that the enemy would soon be coming from the sea.

Everything was ready for them. Along the kilometre-long front two lines of barbed wire ran, the second one two metres high. In front of them, dug into the side of the sea wall, the forward artillery observers scanned the still green sea with their glasses. Behind the wire in the pre-war boarding houses and hotels now turned into virtually impregnable strongpoints, the infantry tensed with their rifles and machine-guns, waiting for the order to fire from their HQ, the former Casino.

Three miles away in the great concourse of little ships deployed in a wide arc advancing steadily at ten knots an hour towards their own date with destiny, five thousand other men felt a sense of impending crisis. They had come a long way for this date: from the cold, impersonal streets of Canada's eastern cities; the burning summer heat of the western states; the farms; the logging camps; the great lakes apparently as empty and unknown as the day they had been first created. And they had waited, many of them, three years for it. Now finally it was there and suddenly a whole division was gripped by a strange tension. But it was tension greater than was normal among men going into action for the first time. It seemed to grip their limbs in its icy fingers and immobilise them – still their very heartbeats – as if the waiting men already knew that this would be the first and only time. For they were going to their deaths, each and every one of them.

As if some invisible hand had thrown a gigantic power switch, a great flash of light split the sky and the great bombardment started. Naval guns roared, mortars belched, rockets raced across the sky trailing fiery sparks behind them. Red, white, green tracer zipped across the still water, and all around the great arc of vessels flares hushed into the air, as the God of War drew his first fiery breath.

'*Achtung!*' the German NCOs bellowed excitedly. Men took aim. Officers blew their whistles and as the first cumbersome landing craft appeared from the smoke of war, the forward artillery observers began to talk rapidly into their phones.

'*Feuer!*'

As the ramps crashed down and the first khaki-clad figures started on their mad dash up the steep shingle, the snipers opened up at carefully selected targets. Officers, signallers, NCOs crashed to the wet shingle. Within minutes half the officers of the first wave of the Royal Regiment of Canada were dead and dying, a matter of mere yards from the landing craft.

The Royal Hamiltons got as far as the first line of wire. The new blast of fire stopped them dead, leaving them hanging and trapped on the wire like so many scarecrows who twitched weakly every time a new bullet hit their defenceless bodies. The Royal Highland Light Infantry of Canada charged into the hail of death. Boxed in on all sides by the screaming steel, they fought their way desperately up the beach. Within minutes the first two companies had been reduced to shaken, battered, little groups of men, their officers killed or wounded, taking orders from anyone who cared to take command.

The plan had been to land four troops of the new Churchill tanks in the first wave. But as the six tank landing craft of the Calgary Scottish loomed up from the smoke the defenders concentrated their artillery fire on the cumbersome craft as if they were aware of the deadly cargo they bore. On their decks, the machine-gunners of the Toronto Scottish sacrificed themselves by the score, trying to fight off the enemy with their pathetic Vickers machine-guns. As the craft heeled and reeled under shell after shell, the bodies of the Scottish piled up on their decks like sandbags.

Tank Landing Craft 145, riddled like a sieve, her ramp smashed, her engine room ablaze, reached the beach. But she only had time to land three of her Churchills before she sank. Tank Landing Craft 127, ablaze from stem to stern, her crew dead, a lone rating at her helm, two surviving Toronto Scottish gunners defending her as best they could, staggered into the beach and began unloading her cargo. The Churchills started to clatter out of the burning oven.

Lieutenant Colonel John Andrews, Commanding Officer of the Calgary Highlanders, watched the slaughter of his battalion with an ashen face, his eyes wide and staring. But he knew that there was no time for regret. His own landing craft Number 125 was attracting the full fury of the German fire. Next to her Number 214 was hit once again and began to drift. Andrews' own craft gained some protection in the lee of the stricken vessel, although down on the deck the Brigade Commander Brigadier Lett was severely wounded and next to him Colonel Parks-Smith was dying.

Andrews took a last look at the sky and his own bright battle pennant flying bravely above him and then he clamped down the hatch of the water-proofed tank which could survive to a depth of six-foot of water. As soon as they were within striking distance of that terrible shore he would give the order 'advance'.

The stricken landing craft lurched. The Churchill jerked forward, shot through the ramp and disappeared into eight feet of water. There was a crazy moment of panic as the water started to flood the Churchill's green interior. 'All right, everybody out!' Andrews rapped curtly and the screaming died down.

The men swiftly opened the escape hatches and like submariners coming up from a sunken sub, they surfaced and swam for the shore. Andrews was last out. He clambered on the turret and cried, 'I'm baling out!' Then dived into the boiling, bullet-churned water.

A Navy launch roared in, guns blazing. A gasping, soaked Andrews was dragged aboard. The launch swung round in a wild curve, but was swamped in a deluge of shells. A moment later, engulfed in flames, she sank in the shallows, everyone on board her dead. Only yards away the bright battle pennant continued to fly bravely and as the tide receded, the tank was left high and dry on the wet sand, a mocking symbol of the futility of the whole action.

*   *   *

Not all the Churchills of the Calgary Highlanders were lost on that murderous beach. Dripping with water, machine-guns blazing, a handful of them fought their way across the shingle, crashing down the wire and rattling on to the promenade. The first one was hit by direct fire and skidded to a halt, white smoke pouring furiously from its engine.

Behind it a lone scout car stalled and the next tank rammed its squat snout into its back bumper. All at once the car lurched forward, its crew hanging on for their lives, as it accelerated down the Boulevard Marechal Foch. The Churchill lumbered after it, bursting through the German defences, pouring shell after shell into the hotels and boarding-houses. Several more followed. While the grim slaughter continued on the beaches, the lone scout car and its attendant three Churchills, flying the yellow pennant of the Calgary Highlanders' C Squadron, rattled past the white Casino and disappeared north, heading for the Goebbels Battery.

NINE

'What news, Mountbatten?' Churchill put down his second whisky of the morning and faced the Admiral, with his jaw thrust out pugnaciously. Outside the sirens had died away and the ack-ack was already hammering away in Regent's Park.

'Bad, sir,' Mountbatten answered, taking the seat offered him.

'How bad?'

Mountbatten opened the sheet of paper he had brought with him from his HQ. '*Calpe** reports that at Blue Beach, Puits, there had been no progress. The Royal Regiment of Canada has been virtually wiped out.'

He hesitated and Churchill growled, 'Go on, Mountbatten, give me it all.'

'Sir. At Dieppe itself on Red and White Beaches, the Essex Scottish and the Royal Hamilton Light Infantry are fighting desperately to maintain themselves under steadily increasing fire. We have thrown in all our reinforcements – the Fusiliers Mont Royal and the Royal Marine Commando – and both have suffered very heavy casualties. The only bright spot is that Lovat's* Fourth Commando have destroyed the Hess Battery with relatively light casualties and are already on their way back to England.'

Churchill drained his whisky. Almost automatically he poured himself another one from the bottle on his desk and squirted soda water into it. He didn't offer Mountbatten one, but then he knew the Admiral would have refused anyway: it was only eleven o'clock in the morning. He nursed the drink in

* HQ of the attack force, HMS *Calpe*. (Transl.)
* Lord Lovat, CO of No. 4 Commando. (Transl.)

his hands and asked, 'What of the Goebbels Battery?'

Mountbatten raised his voice above the crack of the anti-aircraft guns firing at another German hit-and-run raider. 'Bad too, sir. Information is scarce, but *Calpe* believes the Commando ran into E-boats. I'm afraid they must have suffered heavy casualties too. In short, sir, the situation is deteriorating rapidly. We must assume that the force will soon have to—,' he shrugged and didn't complete the sentence.

'Withdraw?'

Mountbatten nodded glumly.

'What is your estimate of the casualties?'

'At present, we can only make a rough count. But two hours ago, we believed that half the Canada Division had been killed, wounded or taken prisoner. Perhaps some four to five thousand men.'

The Prime Minister nodded slowly. Outside, the raiders had disappeared. The guns in Regent's Park had ceased firing. Soon the all clear would be sounding and he could go across to the House. 'All right, Mountbatten,' he said carefully, 'you can pull them out. Start Operation Vanquish* – they have suffered enough.'

'Thank you, sir.'

*   *   *

'Why did they do it?' Hitler asked rhetorically, staring at Jodl's pale, clever face. 'Why did they land at Dieppe in the first place?'

Colonel-General Jodl, Hitler's Chief-of-Staff, opened his mouth to speak, but the Führer beat him to it. 'Because, my dear Jodl, that old fox Churchill wanted them to be slaughtered. He wanted to appease the Ivans and prove to that Jew Roosevelt that it couldn't be done. Look at this rubbish.' He put on his steel-rimmed glasses and read swiftly from the

* The Codename for the withdrawal operation from Dieppe. (Transl.)

148

Berlin intercepts of the BBC broadcasts: ' "A raid was launched in the early hours of today on the Dieppe area of enemy Occupied France. The Operation is still in progress and a further communiqué will be issued when fuller reports are available. Meanwhile the French people are being advised by wireless broadcasts that this raid is *not* an invasion." He took a deep breath. 'What pathetic shit!' He bent his head again. 'Or this: Communiqué Number Two. "The troops taking part in the raid on the Dieppe area have landed at all points selected. Heavy opposition was encountered in some places, and on the left flank one landing party was initially repulsed but reformed and later carried the beach by assault. The troops on the right flank, having achieved their objective, which included the complete destruction of a six-gun battery and ammunition dump, have now been re-embarked. In the centre tanks were landed and heavy fighting is proceeding –" ' he broke off and dropped the intercepts contemptuously on the floor.

Jodl bent and picked them up again; he was by nature a very tidy man.

'How puerile!' Hitler cried. 'Do the Tommies really have to send in a whole division of infantry to blow up half a dozen guns? And why land a whole battalion of their latest tanks on a *raid*, I ask you Jodl? ... No, Churchill's hand has been forced. He deliberately planned this raid right from the start so that it would fail. I mean, why did Canaris's* people get to know of it so easily in England in May?' He stopped. 'My God,' he breathed. 'Oh, my God!'

'What is it, my Leader?'

'Do you think that – no, it is not possible! Even that whisky-swilling cynic could not be that cold-blooded!'

'Cold-blooded as what?' Jodl asked dutifully.

'As cold-blooded as,' Hitler's voice was full of awed admiration, *'to leak the whole operation to us from the very start!'*

* Head of the German Secret Service. (Transl.)

TEN

The German positions were silhouetted harshly against the red disc of the sun, every detail revealed. Here and there scarlet flame stabbed the blackness in hesitant confusion. For even after an hour of their sniping and occasional mortaring, the Germans at the Goebbels Battery had not pin-pointed the direction from which the eighteen-man attack was coming.

The Laird of Abernockie and Dearth fired once again, felt the satisfying slap of the rifle butt against his shoulder and saw the spurt of fragmented stone where his bullet struck the concrete next to the firing slit of one of the guns. 'Right up the Kyber!'

'Fanny's drawers!' one of his men commented. 'Wouldn't get much for that on the range, sir.'

The Colonel grinned. 'I suppose you're right, Curtis. But still it keeps their big squareheaded noggins down and so far the buggers haven't fired those nasty popguns of theirs!'

'I wonder why not, sir?' the Snotty, sprawled next to him in the pit, asked.

'I don't know exactly, laddie. But I can guess.'

'Yes?'

'Something's gone wrong with op and the Navy's not coming in as close as was anticipated,' the Laird replied, casually firing again at the white blur of a face that had suddenly revealed itself at the slit.

The blur disappeared and Curtis cried, 'Bullseye, sir.'

'Yes,' said the CO, 'not bad for a little bloke like me, I must admit.'

'Then why are we hanging on here, sir?' continued the Snotty. 'I mean don't think I'm windy, sir, or anything like

150

that, sir, but I just wonder what purpose we're serving here if the battery's not going to fire at our people.'

'I know you're not scared, lad, and even if you was, we all are, you know, but the evacuation is scheduled to start at thirteen hundred hours. Okay, then the Royal will have to start really coming close to shore to cover it and you can imagine that the Jerries won't miss a target like that.' He shrugged easily and fired again an instant later. 'I think it's then that we really can come in useful.'

'And after that, sir?' the boy persisted.

'Grr, you ain't half a worrier, laddie! After that, it's anybody's guess what'll happen. You know what they say, if me Auntie Fanny had a moustache she'd be me Uncle Joe. Let's worry about that one when the time comes.'

But the time had already arrived. The Laird had hardly spoken the words when the first Spitfires came zooming in at 400 mph and at tree-top height. They hurtled round and round over the coast to the left of their attackers, the smoke cannisters tumbling from their lean bellies in crazy confusion. Almost at once a great screen of white smoke began to ascend to the sky. The red ball of the sun was blotted out and the front of the battery was blanketed with the start of the smoke screen.

It was the signal the German gunners had been waiting for, it seemed. A zinc-coloured light blinked at the furthermost turret. An orange flash, a great wild puff of black smoke. A crazy tearing noise struck the air.

'There the buggers go!' yelled the Laird and opened his mouth automatically, as the hot blast whipped against his face. 'Come on, lads, let's see what we can do. Aim right for the slit, as the actress said to the bishop!'

They set to work with a will, directing a steady stream of rifle and machine-gun fire towards the apertures of the great guns. Concrete flew everywhere. Bullets whined mournfully. They could hear the regular thump-thump of the mortar bombs landing on yet another turret, sending chunks of stone hurtling in every direction. Yet the enemy guns continued to fire.

The Laird lowered his rifle. 'Bugger this for a tale! This ain't doing no good at all!' For a moment he crouched there on his heels, while Curtis at the Spandau poured a stream of fire into the German positions. Then he came to a decision. 'Snotty,' he yelled, 'you're in charge here for a mo. I'm gonna have an O group* with me second-in-command.'

Without waiting to see the young sub-lieutenant's reaction, he grabbed his rifle by the barrel and crouched low, doubled across the rough ground to the pit occupied by Freddy Rory-Brick and his men.

'Freddy,' he gasped, diving in beside the hatless Guardsman, 'sod this for a lark, we're doing about as much good here as one of each waiting for vinegar.'

'What?' Freddy yelled above the roar.

'Bloody hell, can't you speak English! I said we're bloody well wasting our time here. So far we've kept 'em in their turrets all right, but now we're not stopping them firing.'

'Agweed, sir, but what do you suggest?'

'Concentrate and have a bash at one of the buggers. All or nothing. If we take the turret, then we're in business. We can have a go at the others with its gun.'

'Wisky, sir?'

'Of course, it's sodding *wisky*! It's *wisky* crossing the road in the Big Smoke. It's *wisky* bending down to pick up a feather – yer can knacker yersen that way. So what? You don't want to live for ever, do you, Freddy?' He nudged him affectionately. 'Eh?'

Freddy smiled. 'I'm with you, sir.'

'Good, no time for fancy tactics. We go in from three sides. If we're lucky, they'll be too busy with their popguns to notice us. If we're unlucky, I'm sure we'll make lovely corpses. Are you on?'

* Officers Group, ie conference. (Transl.)

'On, sir!'

Five minutes later the little band of commandos were ready. The Laird waited tensely until he saw the gun of the turret they were going to storm raise its barrel prior to firing at the unseen ships once again. 'Get ready!' he yelled.

The men clasped their weapons even tighter in hands that were wet with sweat.

The Laird raised himself to one knee, his ragged, torn kilt hanging in the dust.

The gun thundered. '*Now!*' he cried above the deafening noise.

The commandos streamed forward, firing from the hip at an enemy safely ensconced behind his foot-thick concrete defences. They caught the gunners off guard. By the time they had begun to react, the commandos were already within the shelter of the turret-wall.

'Down!' cried the Laird above the crackle of surprised, frightened enemy fire, 'get down! Round the back!'

The men bent double below the level of the enemy firing slits and pelted after him to the rear of the turret. A large metal door stopped them. The Laird grabbed the handle and threw it open. Menzies just behind him knew the drill without having to be ordered. He threw in his last grenade and the Laird slammed the door shut again. There was a thick, muffled crump, and smoke streamed out of the nearest slit. They heard the sound of glass shattering somewhere.

The Laird threw a glance behind him. Freddy was in position, Tommy gun at the ready. 'Now!' he yelled and threw the door open again.

Splay-legged, body crouched, Freddy poured a vicious hail of fire into the smoking gloom. The artillerymen, screaming and terrified, faces black with smoke, a few of them suffering from multiple wounds, walked straight into the bullets.

The commandos scrambled frantically over their writhing bodies. The bunker stank of sweat and cheap tobacco – even the acrid smell of cordite couldn't hide that. For a moment they stood there in the gloom, hesitant, wondering which passage to take.

'Stwaight ahead,' Freddy suggested.

'Right!' the Laird drew his skean dhu. 'Come on lads, here we go again!'

A soldier in his undershirt appeared from a door on the right. He had a pistol in his hand but he never managed to fire it. The little knife hissed through the air and caught him directly in the chest. His knees gave way beneath him and he sank to the floor. Menzies kicked him in the face as he ran by.

The Laird threw open the metal door which barred their way. Light streamed out from the caged electric bulbs in the ceiling to reveal the gleaming breech of the gun and the naked sweating backs of the gunners bent over the huge shell they were loading.

The commandos fired, the noise of their rifles making an ear-splitting din in the confines of the bunker. The gunners hadn't a chance. Their naked upper bodies were riddled with bullets as they dropped to the concrete floor all around the breech.

'Look out, sir!' screamed Curtis frantically.

Freddy Rory-Brick took the burst in the stomach. At that range it threw him round like a dancer executing a turn. He grabbed wildly for the support of the wall, but his strength failed him. His hands clawed the length of the wall, his nails breaking, trailing a smear of blood behind them.

'*Kamerad! ... Bitte, Kamerad!*' called the bespectacled gunner who had shot Freddy from the corner where he had hidden, and dropped his schmeisser.

'*Fuck Kamerad!*' the Laird hissed, beside himself with rage. He picked up the Tommy gun which had fallen from Freddy's nerveless fingers and fired a mad burst into the terrified gunner.

At last, when the German was a mutilated corpse on the

154

floor, the Laird dropped the tommy gun and turned to Freddy.

The Snotty had propped him up against the wall, while the others cleared the dead Germans from the gun.

'I'm afwaid,' Freddy gasped painfully, his face the colour of clay, the end of his nose already pinched and waxen, 'I've . . . bought a bad one . . .'

'Ballocks!' the Laird snapped angrily. 'Don't even talk that kind of codswallop!' Hastily he bent to one knee and fumbled with the blouse of the Guardsman's battledress. He ripped open his blood-soaked, silken khaki shirt and saw that the burst had ripped open Freddy's chest. Through the huge hole he could see splintered white bone among the red mess and the pale grey of his viscera pulsating obscenely. He recoiled, unable to hide the look of horror in his eyes.

'That bad?' Freddy inquired weakly but calmly.

'Of course not, Freddy.' The Laird ripped open his field dressing and placed it over the gaping wound. It was no use. The yellow lint soaked through almost immediately. The Laird stared down at it helplessly.

'Give my love to my wife and the boy,' Freddy said faintly, his eyelashes fluttering.

'Cor ferk a duck, Freddy, you'll live to give it to 'em yerself,' the Colonel lied.

'Do you weally think so . . .' Major the Hon Frederick Oakley Rory-Brick's head flopped to one side. His mouth dropped open and he was dead.

It was just then that Curtis, peering through the observation slit, cried excitedly. 'Tanks, sir! Our tanks – they're Churchills!'

ELEVEN

C Troop of the Calgary Highlanders caught the survivors of the Wotan's Third and Fourth companies just as they had begun their advance out of Belleville behind the cover of the two Mark IVs which had finally freed them from the trap. One moment the hundred or so shaken youths, urged on by the Vulture's vitriolic tongue and the kicks of the veteran NCOs, had been in clear sunlight; the next they were sealed in the grey gloom of the smoke screen, confronted by the frightening bulk of the three squat Churchills.

The Canadians were as surprised as the SS. They, too, were experiencing their first taste of battle, but they had three years of training behind them and reacted quicker and better than the Wotan crews.

They immediately took up the hull-down position. The SS tankers reacted the way inexperienced crews always did. Confident that their 75mms could outgun the short six-pounders of the Churchills they swung their turrets round, but forgot they were exposing the whole length of the tanks to the enemy fire.

'*Cretins!*' the Vulture raged, while all around him his men scrambled for cover. 'Offer them your glacis plate.'* In his fury at the inexpert way the Mark IVs were being handled, he lashed his riding crop against his boot. 'Great crap on the Christmas Tree – give them the glacis!'

But the eager young tankers rattling into action did not hear him.

'Then die, you idiots!' the Vulture cursed and threw his

* The most heavily armoured part of the tank to its front. (Transl.)

cane at the ground.

The two Mark IVs fired the first shots. Their long, hooded guns squirted scarlet flame. Both shells struck the little armoured car as it scuttled for cover. It slithered to a sudden stop and slumped to one side in flames.

'My God!' the Vulture gasped, hardly believing it possible that men could be so stupid; they were using high explosive shells instead of armour-piercing ones needed for tank combat. 'AP,'† he screamed, his face scarlet. '*Use AP!*' he pulled out his pistol and fired a volley of furious shots at the rear of the Mark IVs.

But already it was too late. While the inexperienced gunners madly cranked round their 75s to bring them to bear on the hull-down Churchills, the three tanks fired.

The closest Mark IV reared up like a live thing as the shell caught it in the boogies. The second shell struck it. The whole tank trembled violently. Frantically the young, panic-stricken crew fought to get out before the tank went up in flames.

Again the Canadians were more experienced. They were waiting for the move. Three Besa machine-guns spoke as one, concentrating on the stricken Mark IV. The driver took a full burst in the chest and flopped down in his hatch again. The commander and the gunner managed to get out of the turret, but were killed before they could spring from the deck.

The Vulture grunted. 'Serves the damned fools right!' he exclaimed and watched how the second Mark IV reeled from side to side like a ship in a storm, as the Canadians pounded it with shell after shell. In his fear, the driver reversed blindly, and crashed the tank into its burning companion. The gleam-ʒ steel scars which the AP fire had gouged in its sides glowed bloodily in the flames. But only for an instant for the flames had spilled on to the other tank. A hand clawed its way out of the turret, a hand already charred black, dripping burning flesh. As it poised there it looked as though the black bones

† Armour piercing shells. (Transl.)

157

were extended to heaven, pleading for mercy. But there was no mercy for the trapped crew. The tank exploded in a burst of bright, oil-tinged flame.

The Vulture ducked hastily as a severed boogie hurtled just above his head. When he raised his head again, the Mark IV had disappeared with nothing to mark its passing except for a patch of scorched earth.

The Vulture was not concerned with the fate of the inexperienced tankers. His concentration was fixed on the Churchills which had already disappeared again into the smoke screen. He cursed bitterly and rose to his feet, for he knew instinctively where they were heading. Now he had three damned Tommy tanks between him and the Goebbels Battery.

TWELVE

Under the cover of the Spitfires and Hurricanes sweeping low over the burning town, machine-gunning the suddenly triumphant Germans, the survivors started to withdraw, falling back slowly to the mile-long, scimitar-shaped beach, the heart of the bloody battle for Dieppe. Out at sea the little boats pressed closer and closer, Oerlikons pumping away at the Focke-Wolfes sneaking in from the land. Behind the little ships, the destroyers swept as near as they dared and in the hull-down position pumped shell after shell into the outskirts of the town where they knew the Germans were.

The beach itself was still hell. Everywhere lay the ripped remnants of shattered tanks and beached, burnt-out landing craft, behind which the survivors, wounded and unwounded, sheltered as best they could, still returning the enemy fire. Behind them the water was full of the debris of battle and men, some of them floating face downwards, still in their life preservers.

By now the tide had begun to ebb. This meant that not only would the survivors have to cross two hundred yards of beach swept constantly by murderous fire, they would also have to wade out a further fifty through the shallows until they reached the boats. HMS *Calpe* ordered the destroyers to go closer.

The German bombers seized their chance. Breaking through the smoke of battle which lay across the sea off Dieppe, three Dornier bombers fell on the destroyer *Berkeley*. The slim rakish destroyer was named after Admiral Berkeley, who two hundred and fifty years before had reduced Dieppe to ashes*

* In 1694. (Transl.)

with his fleet. Now it was the turn of the ship bearing the long dead Admiral's name to suffer the same fate.

A Spitfire zipped across the sky, eight machine-guns chattering. One of the pencil-slim, two-engined Dorniers broke its dive, jettisoned its bombs uselessly in the sea, yards away from the destroyer. But the other two pressed home their attack. Their bombs hit the destroyer amidships, shattering the bridge. Wing-Commander Skinner, the official RAF observer, watching the start of the rescue operations through his binoculars, was killed immediately. His friend, the US Army Air Corps observer, Lieutenant Colonel Hillsinger was blown off the bridge on to the forward deck, where he stared in both anger and awe at the bloody stump where once his right foot had been.

Minutes later HMS *Berkeley* disappeared beneath the waves.

The defenders of the perimeter began to give way, forced back relentlessly by ever-increasing German pressure. The handful of Rangers still alive who had been attached to the commandos, surrendered. But they were still defiant. Excited by their capture of the first Americans they had seen, the Germans asked one tall bareheaded Ranger: 'How many American soldiers are there in England?'

The Ranger looked down contemptuously at his captors and drawled in his Texan accent: 'Three million. And they're all as tall as me. Shit, they have to keep 'em behind barbed wire to stop them swimming the Channel to get at you bastards!'

Another group of French-Canadians, the sole survivors of a company of the Fusiliers Mont Royal, surrendered under the command of their sergeant. The Germans disarmed them and forcing them to strip to their underclothes and boots, made them face a wall with their hands in the air.

But their sergeant, Dubuc, had now regained his second wind after the fighting of the morning. Carefully he tried to work out how many of the German patrol which had captured

them had moved on deeper into Dieppe. In the end he estimated they were being guarded by exactly one German.

Dubuc let his head slump to one side, as if he were utterly
weary and dejected. From this angle, he could watch the
solitary guard, his rifle pointed at the backs of his prisoners,
his eyes continually flickering towards the burning front.

The sergeant gave a soft groan and seemed to collapse
against the wall. 'Water,' he croaked piteously. 'Please,
water!'

The German took a step forward, caught off guard. Dubuc
dived forward. As the German stumbled to the ground,
Dubuc's hands went round his neck and strangled him.

Dubuc rose to his feet, breathing very hard. But when he
spoke, his voice was calm. 'Go,' he commanded in French.
'Back to the beach. It's every man for himself now.'

The men disappeared into the mass of smoke-shrouded back
streets, trotting through them in their singlets and shorts like a
group of runners who had unexpectedly found themselves in
the middle of a battle.

Dubuc reached the burning beach alone. He found his
Colonel wounded and lying on the sand. After reporting and
excusing his unmilitary appearance, he gathered the CO up in
his arms and began the long perilous passage to the waiting
boats.

The Essex Scottish began to withdraw as a formation.
Throwing the last of their smoke grenades over the esplanade
wall to cover their retreat, they picked up their wounded and
braved the two hundred yards of hell. Like grey ghosts they
staggered through that tormented wasteland, taking casualties
all the time in the withering German fire, brushing past the
dead bodies of their comrades hanging on the wire like bundles
of wet rags, dodging gratefully behind the cover of shattered
tanks that loomed up suddenly out of the shroud of smoke.
Some of them reached the water. They started to wade
through the shallows, blindly scrambling through the green

water, brushing aside the mess of battle-equipment, vomit, bodies, severed limbs – wide staring eyes seeing only one thing – the boats.

Some of them reached them and were dumped in the confused mess of the transports. The quick and the dead thrown together in crazy promiscuity, lay side by side on the open decks of the ships: shivering black-faced men in oil-soaked khaki, eyes dazed by the swiftness of the disaster and their rescue; sailors retching the black fuel oil, with which their lungs were filled; the cruelly wounded, crying out for help to harassed doctors and medics who were now beginning to run out of supplies; the fresh dead being rolled over the side like logs of wood, heads lolling obscenely to make room for more and more wounded. And over the whole terrible scene hung the heavy stench of cordite, fuel oil and blood.

*　　*　　*

The Canadian HQ retreated from the Casino, which had covered the withdrawal to the beaches as best it could so far. The senior surviving Canadian officer Brigadier Southam refused to be evacuated. Still in radio contact with HMS *Calpe*, he was determined to rescue every man if possible. Crouched behind the wall of shingle at the head of the beach he set up a new HQ, harassed all the time by enemy fire, his commands drowned by the roar and snarl of the ferocious dog-fight between the RAF and the *Luftwaffe* now being waged above the beaches.

By now a thousand men, half of them wounded, had been rescued. But the Germans were closing in on all sides, and the naval commander Captain Hughes-Hallett on HMS *Calpe* knew that it wouldn't be long before the *Luftwaffe* and the heavy guns of the Goebbels Battery started ranging in on his naval force. Nevertheless, he knew from Southam's radio messages, that the Royal Hamiltons were still fighting at Pourville and that at Blue Beach, a company-strength group of Canadians were still holding out against all the Germans could throw at them, as were odd pockets of infantry all along the embattled shore.

Yet time was running out rapidly. He had to make a decision. He called Commander McClintock who was running the rescue operation to him and ordered him to make a personal reconnaissance of the situation.

At twenty minutes past twelve, Commander McClintock signalled Hughes Hallett: 'No more evacuation possible!'

On board the *Calpe*, the Canadian staff officers pleaded with Hughes-Hallett to wait a little longer. Two brigades of the Canadian Division had been shattered, with the loss of all their senior officers. They could not bring themselves to leave Dieppe and abandon the leaderless survivors to their fate. But Captain Hughes-Hallett was adamant. Reluctantly he signalled Commander McClintock: 'If no further evacuation possible withdraw!'

The evacuation fleet began to assemble hastily under the cover of smoke, an umbrella of fighters above them, trying to protect them from the German dive-bombers. Meanwhile Hughes-Hallett made one last attempt to weigh up the situation for himself.

At ten minutes to one precisely, HMS *Calpe* came out of the smoke cover, her sharp prow cleaving the water, all her four-inch guns firing as if she wished to challenge the whole weight of the German military machine. The Germans answered the challenge readily. Steaming broadsides along the length of that long beach, weaving in and out of the incessant German shell-bursts with spouts of churning white water washing over her decks, the *Calpe* braved the furious enemy barrage.

The beach was a scene of tortured desolation; it looked as if some elemental force had swept along it, scooping out huge hollows, flinging the petty man-made machines of war from side to side, as if they were toys, tossing the bodies of men

163

high into the air and smashing them down again on to the cruel shingle limp and dead.

Captain Hughes-Hallett shook his head sadly. HMS *Calpe* swung round, her screws churning furiously, and disappeared back into the smoke screen.

Ten minutes later, all hope gone now, Brigadier Southam sent his final signal. More and more enemy troops were being detrained from Dieppe railway station; the first of his surviving Canadians were beginning to surrender.

THIRTEEN

The three Churchills of the Calgary Highlanders' C Squadron rattled triumphantly towards the Goebbels Battery, unaware that their effort was to no purpose. Through a hole in the smoke screen, the leading tank commander caught a glimpse of the battery with one turret apparently firing at the others. He understood immediately. 'Say guys,' he cried excitedly over the radio to the rest of the troop, 'the commandos must have gotten one of the Jerry guns! Let's go in and give 'em a hand!'

*   *   *

Von Dodenburg, cautiously leading the advance through the smoke behind Schulze's Mark IV, heard them first and knew immediately that they were the enemy.

'Down!' he whispered rapidly, as the rattle of the advancing tanks grew louder. The company flopped simultaneously into the drainage ditch at the side of the road leading to the Battery and took up their defensive positions. Von Dodenburg doubled forward, grabbed hold of the towing hook at the back of the Mark IV and swung himself aboard. Swiftly he clambered up on the turret.

'What's burning, sir?' Schulze asked cheerfully, looking up at his dirt-streaked face from within the green-glowing turret.

'Tanks – enemy tanks,' von Dodenburg gasped. 'Look!' he pointed at the squat shapes beginning to emerge from the smoke.

'Ouch, my aching eggs!' Schulze exclaimed, 'three of the bastards!' Hastily he pressed his throat mike. 'Matzi, head for that rise at two o'clock! Move it! Get yer skates on!' He dug his elbow into the corporal, as the tank increased speed. 'All right, you Hitler Youth hero, park your heroic keester behind that pop-gun. Sergeant Schulze is going to win you the Iron Cross third class this day.' He swung round and looked inquiringly at von Dodenburg.

Despite his weariness and anger, von Dodenburg grinned. 'All right, you big waterfront rogue, you're in charge. Button her up, I'm going.' He ran to the edge of the Mark IV. 'And play it carefully. Don't get your turnip blown off!' He dropped lightly over the side.

'Don't worry yourself, sir,' Schulze shouted after him, as the tank rolled up the little hill, 'Mrs Schulze's favourite son ain't gonna let some buck-teethed Tommy put an explosive enema up his peace-loving arse!'

*   *   *

'Driver halt!' cried the leading Canadian tank commander hurriedly as they emerged from the fog and he spotted the German tank in the hull-down position behind the little hill, its long, hooded gun pointing directly at the advancing troop. 'Traverse left ... two hundred yards,' he ordered. 'Jerry tank ... *Fire!*'

The Churchill jerked to a halt. Next moment it shook with the shock of the six pounder firing. The smoke swept away and the Canadian could see the white glow of the tracer shell as it curved upwards slightly and slowly, before plunging down. To the right of the German's turret, the steel glowed a sudden dull red.

'Jesus H Christ, you've hit him, Charley!' cried the tank commander exuberantly.

'The bastard won't brew though!' shouted the sweating gunner, adjusting his sights frantically. 'I'll try to get in the joint between the turret –'

The German 75mm spurted flame. The Churchill rocked violently. A hot acrid blast wave swept through the turret, slapping the commander and the gunner against the wall. The commander shook his head, bemusedly, then recoiled in horror. In the smoking shambles of wrecked equipment at his feet lay a Negro's head.

Beside him Charley giggled hysterically. 'Rod –' he meant the driver, whose headless body was still propped up in its seat, both hands gripping the steering rods – 'looks like goddam Al Jolson!'

The tank commander pulled himself together. His face blanched with horrified disgust; he kicked the blackened head into the bottom of the tank, where small tongues of blue flame were already licking out greedily for the main ammunition storage bin. 'Bale out, Charley!' he screamed fervently. 'For Chrissake, bale out!'

The two of them scrambled frantically out of the burning turret. Gasping hysterically, they dropped over the side, straight into Major von Dodenburg's fire. They died without even knowing who had killed them.

*   *   *

'Now the next bastard!' Schulze cried excitedly.

The corporal, bleeding from the wound in his cheek looked at him numbly, as Schulze rammed home another shell. 'Eh?' he queried dully.

Schulze punched him in the ribs. '*In*,' he rapped, as the breech slapped close.

'*On*,' the corporal retorted. Through his sight, the next Churchill was neatly outlined against the cross-wires.

'*Fire!*' commanded Schulze.

The gunner squeezed the firing bar. Next to him, peering through the periscope, Schulze automatically opened his mouth against the blast so that his eardrums would not burst. The Mark IV jerked back on its rear sprockets. Acrid smoke filled the turret. The blast wave slapped Schulze across his face. He blinked and heard the clatter of the shell case as it

167

tumbled, hot and smoking, to the deck.

Two hundred yards away, the second Churchill had come to a halt too, a gleaming silver hole skewering its side.

Schulze rammed home another shell and slapped the breech lever up. '*In*,' he cried.

'*On!*'

'Kill the bastard this time – *Fire!*'

The corporal jerked back the lever. The gun erupted. The shell struck the Churchill squarely in its fuel tank. A sole Canadian dropped from the turret, his overalls a mass of blue flame. Von Dodenburg's machine-pistol chattered. The Canadian jerked convulsively and then was still. The flames began to eat his body away.

The third Churchill began to reverse into the smoke screen, its commander firing the smoke grenades on the turret as it went. But Schulze, his blood up now, was not going to be cheated of his prey. 'Matzi –'

'I know!' the one-legged driver thrust home low gear.

The Mark IV clattered into the white gloom after the Churchill, its 75mm turning cautiously from side to side in a forty degree arc, as it sought out its prey.

* * *

A hundred yards away, the commander vehemently cursed the frightened driver. 'You mother-loving, chicken sob!' he yelled angrily, as the Churchill swayed from side to side on the rough ground. 'What in Sam Hill did you wanna go and do that for? We could have took the bastard!'

The driver wasn't listening. The sweat stood out on his brow in petrified beads, his wide staring gaze was fixed on the smoke behind them, fearful that the German tank might appear at any moment and slaughter them as it had done the rest of the troop.

'I order you to stop and fight!' his commander cried, beside himself with rage.

168

'Yeah, for Chrissake, Slack-Ass,' the gunner added, 'knock it off, willya? I can pin his ears back for sure with the six-pounder.'

'Here it comes!' the driver screamed. 'To the left!'

The commander pressed his eyes to the periscope and saw the Mark IV looming up out of the smoke less than a hundred yards away, its 75mm pointing away from them; it had not yet spotted the fleeing Churchill.

'Driver – *halt!*'

Nothing happened. The Churchill continued to bump over the rough cliff-top.

'Joe, in the name of heaven fire!' the commander yelled in despair, fumbling for his 38, 'before the bastard sees us.'

Furiously the gunner spun the turret. The Mark IV slid into his sights, blacking out everything else, it filled his whole world. He could see the great black and white cross, the silver-gleaming shell-hole, every rusty rivet, every oil-dirtied bolt. Holding his breath unconsciously, he raced the wheel of the range drum until it registered one hundred yards.

'On,' he snapped.

'Joe, I order you to halt,' cried the commander, poking his revolver between his big boots in the general direction of the driver's head below, 'or I swear to God, I'll blow the back of your goddam yellow head off!' He clicked back the hammer.

'Hurry!' the gunner urged fervently, 'they still haven't spotted us!' Still no reaction. 'All right, you rotten bastard, take this!' He pressed the trigger.

In those close confines, the revolver's explosion sounded like cannon fire. The gunner lunged instinctively at the firing lever. The unsuspecting Mark IV disappeared from the round circle of gleaming glass sight as if dragged away by an invisible hand, and a moment later the six pounder's shell whistled harmlessly into the air, well above the Mark IV, as with the dead driver's foot jammed down firmly on the gas pedal, the

169

Churchill sailed over the edge of the cliff, her crew screaming helplessly, and crashed into the sea a hundred feet below.

*   *   *

'By the docked dick of the Great Rabbi!' Matz breathed out in a long, awed sigh, as the shell fired by the last Churchill whizzed harmlessly past them to explode somewhere beyond the Battery, 'that nearly parted our hair for us!'

'I can't even move,' Schulze agreed in low voice. 'If I did, it would start dripping down me leg!'

Behind them in the smoky gloom, Von Dodenburg rose to his feet and commanded in a low voice heavy with weariness. 'All right, on your feet, men! Advance, we're nearly there now.'

FOURTEEN

The Laird sadly watched the last Churchill disappearing into the smoke, leaving behind the two burning wrecks. Instinctively he knew that there would be no further attempt now to break through to them. He sensed too that the whole operation had failed. The RAF had disappeared from the battlefield and from the direction of Dieppe, the sound of firing was dying away.

He sat down on the floor with the rest and told himself that what was left of No. 7 Commando had done its bit. Although the shells they had been firing until the Churchills had arrived on the scene had whizzed harmlessly over the other turrets because they had been unable to lower the big gun sufficiently to hit them, they had prevented the Germans from firing effectively out to sea during the crucial period when the fleet had been assembling for the landing.

The Laird felt very weary. They had been fighting now for over twelve hours. They stank of sweat and cordite. It was over three hours since they had last eaten – a piece of bitter chocolate and a handful of raisins from their iron ration – and they were down to the last drops of water left in their water-bottles. The end, he knew, was not far off.

'What do you think, sir?' asked the Snotty at his side.

The Laird turned and slowly wiped the greasy film of sweat from his brow with the back of his sleeve. 'Usual cock-up, laddie,' he said thickly through scummed lips.

'Do you think we'll get out?'

'No.'

'What if –'

'We won't surrender. Look at them,' he swept his hand

171

around the circle of his men squatting on their heels in the gloom of the bunker. 'Them lads of mine have lived all their lives in the outdoors, the moors, the hills, the fields. What do you think years behind the wire in the bag would do to them? Besides,' his voice rose in determination, 'as long as we hold here we can stop this battery from firing at the Navy boys.'

'I see,' said the Snotty tight-lipped, knowing now that the Laird's words had sealed all their fates.

The Laird opened his mouth to say something to comfort him; then changed his mind. They lapsed into silence and the Laird occupied himself with his own thoughts once again.

He hadn't told the boy the whole truth of course. It wasn't just the guns – it was the massacred Commando. He didn't want to get back to England and start the task of trying to rebuild it with new men. Three years of war had worn him out; he could not face the task of turning green callow youths from the recruiting offices into hardened men. Besides, there were the wives and children of the men who had died left behind on his estate at Dearth. If he survived the war, he would have to face them on every day that dawned and know in his heart that he had been responsible for their men's death. He couldn't stand that prospect.

'Sir.' It was Curtis, standing look-out.

'Yes?'

'Yon Jerries are coming, sir.'

Wearily the survivors of No. 7 Commando rose to their feet and manned the slits.

The Laird peered out. A thin, thoughtful line of men in camouflaged uniforms were walking slowly across the yellow, cropped grass towards the turret, holding their weapons at the port, their eyes fixed on the ground, as if they had lost something. 'SS, lads,' he announced.

'Och, Laird,' Menzies snarled. 'Dinna fash yersen about them slopeheads. We can tackle them laddies with one hand tied behind our backs.'

'Ye ken, Laird,' Curtis added, 'we're behind a bluidy foot of concrete. All them laddies have is a wee bit o' grass in front of them.'

The Laird's lean face lit up. 'Yer right enough there, Jock! Come on, lads. Let's show em what the bash-on boys of Seventh Commando can do!' He took careful aim with his rifle and fired.

*   *   *

'Keep moving,' von Dodenburg shouted above the noisy crackle of fire which had erupted from the turret. 'Keep moving!'

One or two of the Hitler Youth volunteers who had dropped to the parched yellow grass got to their feet and rejoined the line.

'That's right, boys,' von Dodenburg said approvingly. 'As long as you're moving you're safe.' A slug whined through the air close by him and his voice faltered for a moment. 'Once they've got you stopped, you make a nice juicy target for them. Keep moving now!'

He quickened the pace. If the Tommies had a machine-gun in the turret, they'd open up with it any moment now and that would be the end of his advance; they had to be close enough to the turret before that happened to be able to cover Schulze and Matz in the Mark IV when it appeared on the scene.

'*At the double!*' he yelled suddenly, as he spotted the long dark barrel protruding from one of the slits.

The company broke into an awkward trot. The enemy machine-gun opened up almost without warning. A man next to von Dodenburg swayed crazily, screaming through the bright arc of blood gushing from his throat. Von Dodenburg felt it soak his shoulder, wet and hot.

'Come on, you cowards!' von Dodenburg screamed desperately. '*Heaven arse and twine, keep going!*'

But already men were flinging themselves down everywhere

in the shelter of a shallow ditch, fifty metres away from the turret, sobbing and screaming with fear, rage, exhaustion as they hit the ground.

'Oh, you shitty bastards!' von Dodenburg cursed as he saw that the company was bogging down, realising that there was nothing he could do about it. He slumped down with the rest, defeated, knowing that now Schulze and Matz would have to take their chance alone.

* * *

Schulze crawled cautiously back to the Mark IV hidden by the slight rise and rejoined Matz who was ecstatically smoking a looted Canadian cigarette.

'Shit, Schulze,' he exclaimed, taking the tiny stub of the cigarette out of his mouth, 'to have a smoke of this stuff is almost as good as shooting your load. We're in the wrong shitty army—'

'Trap!' Schulze cut him short angrily. 'The CO didn't make it. Those wet-tails of his got within fifty metres and then they wet their knickers. They dived for cover.'

Matz savoured the last of the cigarette taken from one of the dead Canadian tankers and said: 'So?'

'So we've got to face up to that crapping great cannon of theirs on our own lonesome.'

Matz nodded. He knew what Schulze meant. When the CO had planned the attack he had hoped that the infantry might have put the big gun out of commission so that the Mark IV could complete the destruction of the bunker in safety. He lowered the tiny stub of cigarette to the ground and placed his boot on it gently. He breathed two streams of blue smoke out of his nostrils. 'What we gonna do then, Schulze?'

'We'll come in from the right flank over there, firing as soon as we cross the top of the ridge.'

'Why don't you send them a shitting printed invitation that we're coming? They'll spot us straight away.'

'Exactly, you miserable piece of apeshit. That's what I want them to do. I want them to have us fixed as being over here. Once they've spotted us, we'll do a quick retreat, provided that you can sort out reverse gear in time, being the dum-dum that you are.'

'I resent that,' Matz said hotly.

Schulze told him what he could do with his resentment and Matz grinned. 'I can't, Schulze. I've already got a double-decker bus up there.'

'Then we make smoke, blinding the buck-teethed buggers and go like a bat out of hell for their rear into the blind ground. Have you got it?'

'Got it!' Matz answered easily. 'Should I carve a couple of crosses for our graves now with my sabre?'

'I'll carve a cross on your ugly mug in a minute. We can do it all right with a bit of luck and provided that you're nifty enough with that joystick of yours. All right, let's roll 'em! And you,' he added to the corporal standing on the turret, his face deathly pale and streaked with black, congealed blood. 'Fire that popgun of yours as soon as we hit that rise. I'm in charge of the smoke launchers. All right, move it!'

*　　*　　*

'Jerry tank!' the Snotty yelled in sudden fear as the Mark IV breasted the rise to their right, showering soil and sods of grass everywhere.

'On that bloody gun – gildy!' the Laird reacted immediately, 'Curtis, Menzies!'

The men needed no urging. A frenzy of fumbling. The great cannon swung round. Two hundred yards away the tank was rolling down the rise, its cannon already in action.

Curtis flung himself in the gun-layer's seat. There was no time to sight the cannon. The Mark IV was only a hundred and fifty yards away. He snatched crazily at the firing lever. The monstrous weapon erupted with a huge roar. Hot blast

175

whipped their tired faces. The turret flooded with yellow smoke. The Laird gasped as his lungs filled with the acrid blast and staggered to the nearest slit. Where the tank had been a moment before there was a sudden hole of brown steaming earth, and beyond it, thick clouds of white smoke rising swiftly from the ground.

'Did we get it?' the Snotty asked excitedly, staggering over to him, his fear replaced by the thrill of combat.

The Laird rubbed his reddened eyes wearily. 'I don't rightly know, laddie, but it looks like it ... All right?' he commanded, his voice firm again, 'keep a weather-eye on that spot, Curtis and Menzies. I don't want no more of them buggers creeping up on us like that. 'Cos once they've got under the range of that popgun of yours, they've got us by the short arm. With them tank guns, they'll take us apart bit by bit and there's bugger all we'll be able to do about it. So keep yer eyes skinned!'

* * *

'Shit on the shingle,' Matz cursed, his voice thin and seeming very far away. 'Never soddingly well do anything like that to me again, Schulze, or I'll stick that bit of tin you wears round yer neck right up your arse – sideways!' Savagely he rammed home yet another gear and the tank rattled across the uneven ground as if the devil himself were after it.

Schulze slapped his ear. He had hardly been able to make out Matz's words, deafened by the roar of the great shell which had shaken the tank, as if it had been a child's tin toy. Next to him the gunner, who had forgotten to open his mouth when the blast had engulfed him, was bleeding from both nose and ears.

Schulze poked his head cautiously above the turret and tried to make out their position in the white smoke which swirled all around them like one of the thick seafogs of his native Hamburg.

176

'Well?' Matz's voice inquired over the radio.

'Don't worry me, monkey turd. Keep your foot down on the gas pedal that's all and give her all the juice you've got!'

'Look out, sir!' the corporal cried urgently.

'What? Oh Christ on a crutch, we're running out of smoke!' A sudden breeze had come in from the sea and was dispersing the fog to their right; they were heading for the cleared patch at thirty kilometres an hour. 'Matz, watch it!'

But the little one-legged driver had already spotted the danger. Frantically he jerked at the left-hand tiller bar to pull the tank round and out of danger but it was too late. They were already in the open, clearly outlined in the brilliant August sunshine which had suddenly flooded the cliff top. 'Oh Mama,' Schulze moaned to no one in particular, as the great gun began to swing towards them, 'here's where we start looking at the taties from below!'

*   *   *

'In the name of sweet Jesus, get that big bitch round, will yer?' the Laird cried hysterically, as Curtis and Menzies heaved the cannon round. 'Come on, the rest of you, don't stand there like spare dildoes in a convent, lend a sodding hand!'

Curtis flung himself into the gun-layer's seat and left the pushing to the rest. Menzies freed one hand and snapped up the breech lever. 'Away ye go, Jock!' he yelled as the gun reached its maximum traverse.

Curtis thrust his eye against the rubber eye-piece. The Mark IV leapt into view, bisected neatly by the graduated line of the sight. 'I'm going to fire,' he yelled and grabbed for the firing lever. In another second the Mark IV would have vanished into the blind ground.

'Fire, for God's sake!' the Laird screamed in fearful exasperation. '*Fire!*'

Curtis jerked back the lever. Once again the big gun roared

177

into life. Instinctively the Laird blinked. When he opened his eyes again a fraction of a second later, he caught a glimpse of the dark whirling mass of the shell heading straight out to sea and the disappearing metal rump of the Mark IV scuttling for the dead ground.

*   *   *

Schulze took over the 75mm personally, as the Mark IV came to a halt some fifty metres behind and to the right of the silent turret. 'You see, greenbeak,' he lectured the young corporal as he settled himself comfortably in the gunner's seat, 'this is where the real expert comes in. For a job like this, you've got to treat yer gun like yer'd treat a virgin – though I suppose you wouldn't even know how to do that. Soft, gentle, trying not to hurt her, but using a bit of cunning to get her to roll over and open her pearly gates for yer, just as we're going to get that lot over there to open their legs for us.' He fondled the gun lovingly.

'Aw for Chrissake,' Matz complained from below. 'I won't be able to get out of the driving seat if yer go on, talking like that – I'll be wedged in here. What is this – a war or a sodding session at Rosi-Rosi's knocking shop?'

Schulze swung the turret round until the long, hooded 75mm was sighted directly on the turret's nearest slit. His big hand clutched at the firing bar. He took a deep breath and then yelled, using all the English he knew, 'All right, Tommies, it's a long way to Tipperary! And here you go!'

*   *   *

Curtis was blinded by the first shell. He reeled back from the observation slit, his face a myriad of bleeding cuts, as if someone had rubbed it with a wire pan cleaner.

Apologetically he said: 'I'm sorry, Laird. But I think yon shell did fer mah eyes. I canna see. Then as the turret was struck a second time and the gloomy, wildly shaking room was filled with thick choking concrete dust, he sat down carefully in the corner and politely but determinedly refused to be touched.

Next to him, Menzies, his pal, pressed his broad back against the heeling wall and began softly saying psalms.

The terrible pounding continued. After a while the Snotty went mad. At first it was a reserved, English form of madness, and consisted of the boy placing his face in his hands and sobbing quietly. But as that monstrous, close-ranged battering went on and on, he began to scream.

The Laird hit him across the face, but the nerve-wracking screaming went on. Then the Snotty began to chew his tongue, his eyeballs turned back in his head with only a bit of the white showing, the saliva running down his dust-coated contorted face was tinged pink with blood.

'Grab hold of him!' the Laird commanded.

A couple of the commandos seized the boy's arms. The Laird drew his skean dhu, and prising open the Snotty's jaw, slid in the little blade to prevent him biting off his tongue. The trick worked. The boy started to grind his teeth on the steel blade, his body still twitching convulsively, but his cries becoming weaker and weaker until they had fallen to a soft whimper, large tears trickling down his cheeks. The Laird cradled the boy's face in his arms, muttering softly to him all the time until he closed his eyes and died.

*   *   *

'Will the buck-teethed bastards never give up?' cried Matz from below. 'My head's going like a shitty ding-dong bell with the noise. And look at the place, it looks as if somebody has worked it over with a power-shovel!'

Schulze nodded. He had destroyed every slit in front of him and the concrete of the turret was so deeply gouged and scarred with shell-fire that there was little trace of its original shape left. 'They must be shittingly well off their heads to stand that kind of punishment,' he agreed and wiped the dripping sweat from his brow, his face burned from the August sun and the terrific heat of the open turret. He threw a glance at Number One Company sprawled in the parched grass waiting for the turret to surrender. 'All the same, the CO's not going to risk those greenbeaks in a direct attack, Matz,' he explained. 'It's up to us to make the Tommies give in.'

'Yeah, it's allus the old heads who get the dirty work.'

With a sigh, Schulze stowed new shells in the ready bins and swung himself behind the red-hot gun once more. 'All right, you little currant-crapper,' he said, 'you'd better take another aspirin for that turnip of yours. Here we go again.' He jerked the lever and the gun roared into violent life.

'Great God and all his shitty triangles,' Matz cursed, his hands pressed tightly over his bleeding ears, 'how long is this going to go on for?'

*   *   *

The Laird was asking himself the same question as the terrible pounding began again. He looked around the shaking, dust-filled gloom of the turret and knew that his men were at the end of their tether. All of them had sunk into a strange lethargy, their eyes wide and staring, the only sign of the tremendous strain they were under, the nervous tics of their dust-coated faces. In between shells the silence of the turret was only broken by Menzies' low murmur as he repeated over and over again, 'the Lord is my shepherd . . .'

Slowly the Laird levered himself up against the trembling wall and said in a voice that he hardly recognised as his own, 'Lads, I . . . I think we've . . . had it . . .'

It seemed an age before the men reacted. Then slowly they turned their eyes in his direction, and looked at him in dumb expectation.

'Lads, do we surrender?' It seemed an age before they reacted. Then, one by one, they shook their heads.

The Laird smiled slowly and gravely. 'Thank you, lads,' he croaked. He raised his voice. 'On your feet. Come on, you bunch of pregnant penguins, get them fingers out of your orifices – *move it!*

'All right. Them sodding Jerries are not going to take us alive – we're the Seventh Commando, remember! The bash-on boys!' There was iron in his voice now. 'Not a ruddy lot of square-bashing squaddies. Come on now, let's see a bit of swank there. You Murdock, get that tunic of yours buttoned up ... Gilchrist, how often have I told yer, you idle man, that your webbing belt's got to be over yer blouse. Now get it soddingly well seen to, or yer'll be on a fizzer before yer knows what hits yer. At the double, man!'

With fingers that felt as thick as pork sausages, the survivors adjusted their uniforms, pulling down their blouses and canvas gaiters, buttoning up their jackets, tugging at their stocking caps. It was as though they imagined they would hear the tremendous voice of Black Jack, the Commando's Regimental Sergeant Major, now long dead and floating face downwards in the English Channel, crying: 'All right, right-markers, *get on parade*!' and they would tense, legs apart, arms rigid down behind their backs, ready to march on as soon as the next command came – '*Seventh Commando – Seventh Commando, get on PARADE!*'

But now the last command they would ever receive was not to get on parade, but to die. The Laird's lips were red against his dusty face as he snarled, 'All right, what are yer waiting for – *fix bayonets!*'

There was a frenzy of fumbling. The Laird turned and walked smartly down the dark littered corridor, turned the steel catches on the door, his head full of the stirring music of the pipes. The men crowded around him, their bayonets glinting in the faint light.

181

'*Now!*' the Laird yelled, raising his skean dhu high in the air.

*   *   *

'Oh, my holy Christ!' Schulze breathed in awe, as they came stumbling out into the bright sunshine, blinded by the sudden light, but bayonets at the ready, led by a little runt of an officer, dressed in an absurd skirt which dangled around his skinny knees. The corporal raised his schmeisser. Hastily Schulze pushed it to one side. 'Knock it off,' he cried angrily.

'Hold your fire!' bellowed von Dodenburg, only fifty metres away, as his men raised their weapons too. '*Hold your fire, I say!*' his eyes filled with awed respect at these filthy apparitions who had once been men, staggering wearily towards them.

But Sergeant-Major Metzger, aware that he must take some part in the battle for Dieppe before it was too late if he were to retain his position as senior NCO of SS Battalion Wotan, was not listening to such orders. Standing at the back of the truck which had brought him to the scene of the action and sure he was in full view of the Vulture, coming up with the rest of the Battalion, he pressed the trigger of his schmeisser. At that range he could not miss.

'Stop that, Metzger!' cried von Dodenburg. 'For God's sake –' the words died on his lips for it was already too late. All of the English were writhing in their death throes on the ground save the lone figure in the kilt who staggered another few paces before he took the Butcher's last burst in his stomach. The thin knees beneath the overlong kilt gave way and he dropped to the ground. The Laird of Abernockie and Dearth, once known as 'Foxy Fergus', was dead at last. When von Dodenburg turned his body over, he was surprised to see the dead Englishman was smiling.

*   *   *

It was five o'clock. Exactly forty minutes later, Field Marshal Gerd von Rundstedt telephoned the Führer's HQ. His message was short and brutal in its simplicity: *'Mein Führer, no armed Englishman remains on the Continent!'*

FIFTEEN

The setting sun was beginning to slip into the sea. From the land the hard black shadows were stealing in at last to hide the terrible beach. Yet for a few more minutes the setting sun still bathed that scene of death and destruction in its crimson light.

Field Marshal von Rundstedt and his staff officers, standing on the shattered, battle-littered promenade, surveyed it in a profound silence broken only by the soft whimpering of the last of the Canadian wounded. Hardened, professional soldiers as they were – many of them veterans of the mass slaughters of the Western Front in the First War – they were awed and impressed by the sheer degree of the massacre.

Nothing had escaped the defenders' withering fire – neither man nor machine. Everywhere the British dead lay, their big boots sticking upwards or face downwards in the warm sand among the shattered tanks and landing craft – the whole beach as far as the eye could see seemed carpeted with their khaki-clad bodies. And everything was so dreadfully still. Nothing stirred except the sand flies buzzing busily above the dead, and the pathetic, wilted hedge-roses which some of the Canadians had plucked to stick in their helmets as they marched so bravely to their boats only a few short hours before.

Field Marshal von Rundstedt took his eyes from that barren, blasted landscape and said in an old and very tired voice, 'Gentlemen, we cannot consider the operation at Dieppe a local raid. The expenditure in men and material was too great for that.' Wearily he pointed his marshal's baton, given to him personally by Hitler, at one of the shattered Churchills. 'One does not sacrifice twenty or thirty of one's most modern tanks for a raid.'

184

There was a low murmur of agreement from his officers. 'No matter. In our propaganda statements we must now emphasise that the enemy believed he could seize a bridgehead here at Dieppe and then use the good port facilities for bringing up and landing in succession the floating and operational reserves. We shall call it a failed attempt at the Second Front. Is that understood, gentlemen?'

'Understood, Excellency.'

For a few moments the aged Field Marshal was silent, sunk in his own thoughts. His watery gaze fell on a little group of Tommies caught by a burst of fire in the act of setting up a machine-gun. One was still propped up behind his Bren gun by the sand, peering along the barrel, his face set in an eloquent, passionate look of devotion to duty, even in death, with the sand flies crawling over the glassy balls of his eyes. Next to him lay the loader with the curved magazine clutched in his claw of a hand, his lips drawn back in a grim smile that gave his dead face a triumphant look.

'It was an amateurish operation,' he whispered drily to himself. 'One would think they wanted it to fail right from the start.' He shivered.

'Is anything the matter, Excellency?' his chief aide inquired anxiously.

'No, Heinz, it's nothing.' He smiled thinly, his eyes almost disappearing into the mass of wrinkles around his faded eyes. 'A louse must have run over my liver. But I will tell you this, gentlemen,' he raised his thin voice so that they could all hear, 'they will not do it like this again. And they will come again, believe you me!' He took a last look at the still sea, momentarily flushed a dramatic crimson by the dying sun, and turned to go without another word. His staff officers, suddenly depressed and apprehensive, filed after him to the waiting Horch.

*   *   *

'All right, it's all clear,' Schulze whispered, as the staff car with its ancient passenger drew away and the beach was left to the dead, 'he's gone, Matzi.'

Matz, his face still streaked with the sweat of battle and dirt, limped out of the deepening shadows towards his waiting mate. 'Who was it?'

'Rundstedt, I think.'

'He had a face like forty days' rain. You'd think he'd be happy. After all he's just won another victory. It's a bit more to put him in the history books one day.'

Schulze shrugged. 'Victory, do you call it?' He waxed a big paw at the shattered landscape and the waxen faces of the dead.

Matz nodded slowly. Even he was awed by the sight of the thousands of dead Canadians, lying stiff, still and abandoned on that beach. His voice was low as he said, 'Aw come on, Schulze, let's shitting well get on with it.'

In silence, with Matz limping a little behind Schulze's massive bulk, they began to explore that dreadful strand, searching each Service Corps vehicle carefully for what they hoped to find.

'Where there's a shitty Scot, there's shitty Scotch whisky,' Schulze had lectured Matz after the Butcher had mown down the little runt of a Tommy in his ragged skirt and they had realised that he was a Scot, 'and it's up to Mrs Schulze's little boy to find it.' Now the grim sight of the thousands of dead men littering the beach made him regret his decision. Nevertheless he had promised Major von Dodenburg that the depressed, exhausted survivors of the First Company would have their whisky this night before, 'those thieving bastards of base stallions — kitchen-bulls, bone-menders, shit-shovellers and head-hunters — got their flippers on the loot.'

Thus, while the Mark IV rattled along the promenade parallel with them ready to transport back the loot to the waiting youngsters of the First, they combed the beach wordlessly, depressed, trying to avoid looking at those countless, sightless eyes, which somehow seemed filled with reproach at this intrusion.

Finally they found what they sought – an amphibious jeep, bearing the green and white sign of the Service Corps, its axle wrecked, its driver slumped with his bloody head against the shattered windscreen, but with the wooden crates in its back still intact.

'Sabre!' Schulze snapped laconically.

Matz gave him his SS dagger.

Wordlessly Schulze dug his blade under the wooden lid and heaved. It came away to reveal the bottles stacked neatly in their piles to straw.

'Whisky,' Matz said without triumph.

Schulze nodded and putting his thumb and forefinger in his mouth, whistled shrilly. It was the signal for the corporal to halt the tank. With the practised ease of someone who had spent his youth heaving hundredweight sacks of cement at Hamburg's docks, he thrust a case of the whisky into Matz's waiting hands.

Matz set off towards the waiting Mark IV. Far away Schulze could hear the steady tramp of heavy boots. Military police patrol, he told himself, and swung two cases on each shoulder. He caught up with Matz just as he clambered up the sea wall to the tank waiting in the deepening shadows.

'Here,' he grunted and heaved the four cases on to the tank's deck. 'Get that stowed. The headhunters are on their way!'

The corporal thrust the cases down the turret into the eager hands of the new driver. Finally he said, 'what about that one?' He indicated the case still on Matz's shoulder.

Schulze shook his head. 'We're keeping that one for ourselves. Now be off with you, back to those thirsty greenbeaks before the headhunters nab you for looting – and tell the CO he's just granted us two days' special leave in Dieppe for services rendered.'

The corporal opened his mouth to protest; then he changed his mind. Hurriedly he disappeared into the turret and the tank rattled away into the growing darkness. Matz, still clutching the case of whisky in his hands, waited till the roar of its motors had died away, then asked: 'And what was that in aid of, Schulze?'

Schulze took the case from him and deposited it on his own big shoulder. 'Listen carefully, wet-fart, I'm going to explain it simple to you. This whisky's worth a fortune, ain't it?'

Matz nodded.

'So what is Mrs Schulze's little boy gonna do with it?'

'He's gonna flog it on the black market,' Matz replied. 'I know that, you dum-dum. But what are yer gonna do with the green moss you'll get for it?'

'We'll join the Resistance,' Schulze announced and slipped the big thumb of his free hand between two of his dirty fingers in an explicitly obscene gesture.

Matz's wicked little eyes sparkled for the first time since they had first seen that terrible beach. 'You mean Rosi-Rosi's?'

'Right in one, bird-brain. With the Marie we'll get for this firewater, we'll hire the whole shitty place for the next forty-eight hours. Just for me and you, Matzi.'

'Holy strawstack,' Matz breathed, 'what a way to go!'

Schulze's big face hardened for a moment, but only for a moment. 'Yer know what they say, Matzi,' he said seriously, throwing a last glance at the myriad dead now disappearing into the black clutch of the night, 'war's hell, but peacetime –'

'Will shittingly well kill yer!' bellowed Matz. When the MP patrol swung stolidly round the corner, they were already running wildly up the promenade towards the brothel, laughing like crazy men.